# HOLIDAY HORRORS

## AIDEN PIERCE

# A Word of Warning

Cry for Krampus is a dark monster romance containing graphic content that may be triggering for some.

Trigger/Content Warnings: Murder, gore, domestic/spousal abuse, loss of a parent, abandonment, light body horror, violence, monster appendages, size difference, cage play, chain play, foreign object insertion, blood play and other graphic sexual content. Also, note that this is a 24,000-word novella. If you're here for a long holiday read, this isn't it. If you want to read about a woman taking control of her life by giving it to the Krampus in one wild weekend of sin and debauchery, then read on....

*For all the naughty monster fudgers hoping for a visit from the Krampus this holiday season instead of Santa...*

# Chapter One

## Clara

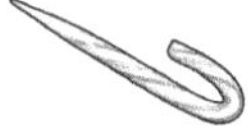

“Get fucked, you stupid piece of—” I tossed the tartan bow I'd spent the last hour trying to tie just right on this Christmas wreath and get the placement just right as the rope of jingle bells attached to my shop's front door announced a customer.

Ignoring the urge to scream and hurl the wreath against the wall, I straightened and greeted them with a smile. "Welcome to Floral Wonderland! Oh... It's you."

My gut twisted when Bastion Weber strode into my shop, the door swinging shut behind him with a festive jingle. Wearing that shit-eating smirk of his, he picked his teeth with the candy cane he was never seen without—always sucked to a deadly point.

"Not exactly a holly jolly greeting, Clara. You greet all your customers like that?"

My smile slipped back into a scowl. "You're not my customer; you're my Christmas tree guy."

Bastion's line of sight dropped to the wreath on my counter, with pine cones and poinsettias scattered around it like a cadaver after a botched operation. "Tough client?"

"This one's for me. I'm going to put it on my car. I just need it to be perfect. Something's off, and I can't put my finger on what."

"It's probably fine. You know how you are."

My eyes narrowed into deadly slits, and I drummed my bright Santa red nails against the counter. "Excuse me? *How I am?* What the hell is that supposed to mean?"

I'd known Bastion since we were little. We'd gone to the same school and were raised in the same little Christmas-obsessed, Krampus-themed town nestled in the Cascade mountains.

The handsome bastard, with coal-black hair and conniving eyes, rubbed me the wrong way. He was the only one in this town who saw through the mask I wore every day.

"You like to obsess over the details because it distracts you from the life you've spent so long pretending is perfect. And that's okay. Just because everyone else in this town is so damn cherry all the time doesn't mean you have to be. Swear all you want, throw all the wreaths. Just don't mind me while I get some popcorn."

"You're a dick," I seethed, turning my attention back to the wreath.

"Come on, Clara," he said, his voice softening with an apologetic cadence. "Jokes aside, I'm being serious. Just because we live in a winter-fucking-wonderland doesn't mean we have to pretend like our lives are perfect."

Easy for him to say.

Bastion had no damn idea of the kind of fresh hell my life was every night I went home to my piece of shit fiancé.

Admitting just how messed up my relationship with Hogan was would quite possibly break me. No. Better to live in a winter wonderland of make-believe. The one that allowed me to pretend my life as a florist, running my own flower shop in the most magical, Hallmark-Christmas-type town, was nothing short of perfect.

"Why are you here?"

He gestured to my shop window, where his truck loaded up with Christmas trees was parked beside the snow-covered curb. "Got one last Christmas tree delivery for you."

"Shipment isn't due for another three days."

Bastion chuckled as he approached my register counter. When his shadow fell over me, I finally looked up from my wreath to see him leering down with a grin. "Decided to drop off the trees early." He paused for a beat before adding, "Got a good batch. Figured I'd let you have it before all the tree lots swooped in."

Just like how he could see right through the sun-shiny, "my life is perfect" persona I put on for everyone, including myself, I saw right through his lies. He was always looking for excuses to come around and check on me.

Maybe I would enjoy his company—he was hot as fuck—if it wasn't for the fact that Hogan hated him. My fiancé was under the impression that my Christmas tree guy had a thing for me.

Maybe he knew that too, and that's why he came around...just to get on Hogan's nerves. I wondered if he'd still do it if he knew just how angry Hogan could get.

"Just leave the Christmas trees out front." I gestured to the wooden caddy his dad had built for the person who'd owned the floral shop before me. Bastion and his family had been running the local Christmas tree farm for decades. When his father passed, Bastion inherited it.

The caddy was looking bare, with only a dried-out tree missing many of its needles. As annoyed as I was that Bastion was here and that Hogan might catch him, I was relieved to get my delivery early.

"Fine. Look, the real reason I came..."

*Because you like pissing my fiancé off by hanging around all the time, and you have no idea the Hell that's brought down on me when another man even so much as breathes in my direction.*

I didn't dare voice the words in my head as I watched him reach into his jacket, pulling out a package wrapped in Krampus gift paper and topped with a silver bow. The wrapping was a design I'd seen often, one that all the souvenir shops on Main Street sold.

Our town was famous for its Krampus lore. Sure, Krampus originated from Germany, but it was said that Bigfoot roamed the other side of these mountains. Krampus sightings among the skiers and hikers over the last century occasionally popped into the papers. Probably too much boozy eggnog. And what else did *The Leavenworth Gazette* have to publish, anyway? It wasn't like our town, with a population of twenty-four hundred, had much else going on.

I eyed the Christmas present he placed on the counter for a beat before pretending to look for a hidden camera. "Am I being punked right now? I thought Bastion Weber doesn't 'do' Christmas."

"I don't. It's not a Christmas present. It's just a gift. Take it."

I blinked. "You've never given me anything before."

"Not true. I gave you my candy cane in the third grade, remember?"

"You mean the one you stole from Tommy Brown and stabbed him with before handing it to me?"

"He bullied you. I made him pay. I'll make any man who hurts you pay, Clara."

Bastion was always protective. Too bad it would take more than a sharpened candy cane to deal with Hogan.

"You don't like Hogan. That's fine. You don't have to. It's really none of your business. You know why, Bast? Because you're my Christmas tree delivery guy."

"I've known you since we were kids. No one else in this town seems to notice how miserable you are, no matter how much you put on that pretty fucking smile, Clara."

"I'm not miserable, asshole."

Bastion's brow furrowed with doubt. He knew I was lying. The third anniversary of my mom's death had just passed, and everyone seemed to know my dad wasn't coming to town for Christmas this year. Again. My dad was busy living up his new life in sunny Florida with his new girlfriend. Everyone in town had gotten his cheesy Christmas card of them posing in an orange grove; he dressed up as Santa with his girlfriend dressed as an elf, pulling two large oranges out of a big red bag labeled "Santa's Sack."

I'd be all alone on Christmas. Well, Hogan would be there, but that just made the whole thing worse.

Bastion's mouth hardened into a line. "Look. Just take the gift, okay?"

I stared at the package with a pit in my stomach. I wanted to take it, but if Hogan found out...

"I can't accept it," I told him with a shake of my head.

"Why?" Bastion challenged, his voice hard and full of ice. He knew the reason, but I'd never confirm it. I couldn't let him or anyone else know that I was terrified of accepting attention from any man who wasn't Hogan.

"I—I didn't get you anything," I replied lamely.

Bastion sighed, shoving his hands in his pockets and pulling out the gloves he wore to unload his trees. I watched him tug them on, trying not to drool at his huge hands and how good they looked wrapped in the bark-roughened leather. "I'm gonna unload the trees."

He turned, leaving the package on the counter. I shouted at him, but he pretended he didn't hear me as he weaved his way through the tables covered in floral arrangements, pots and various planters. When he opened the door, the sound of Christmas carolers from across the street and the clip-clop of hooves from the horse-drawn carriages carried inside.

Bastion shot me a lingering backward glance. It seemed like he was going to say something but thought against it and settled for a smile that appeared to have all sorts of secrets tucked into the corners of his mouth.

"You know I'm not the biggest fan of this holiday. But... Merry Christmas, Clara. If anyone deserves to have a good one, it's you."

"Um, yeah. You too." I pretended to turn my attention back to my wreath, but from the corner of my eye, I watched Bastion unload the trees from his truck and arrange them in his dad's old tree caddy through my storefront window.

Movement drew my eye to the other window, and my heartbeat froze in my chest.

A man wearing a plaid fleece jacket—the one I'd gotten slapped for because I'd bought him the wrong color last Christmas—stood outside the window.

It was Hogan.

By the look of rage on his face, he'd seen Bastion—knowing full well it wasn't a scheduled delivery day—give me the gift.

It would have been such an innocent gesture in anyone else's eyes. But not my fiancé.

Hogan was beyond possessive. He was a fucking psychopath, and not in a fun way like in some of those romances I read to escape my shitty reality. In those kinds of books, the "hero" was almost always the villain who would burn the world down for his woman. Hogan, the hog farmer otherwise known as "The Honied Ham Man" in town since he also opened up a pop-up ham shop during the holidays, was very much a bad guy. But Hogan wasn't like the men in those books.

He wouldn't hurt anyone but me.

# Chapter Two

## Clara

Bastion quickly unloaded the trees and drove off. By then, Hogan had left. Probably off to close up his shop down the block. The lump in my throat grew spikes at the thought of him walking past all the pretty shop windows, all the carolers and vendors selling hot cider and roasted chestnuts as he thought of all the ways he was going to punish me.

Stupid Bastion. He thought he was being protective, but he was just making everything worse. Though, even if Bastion hadn't given me that gift, Hogan would just find some other reason to be jealous. An innocent hello or a head nod from another man could set him off.

I used to think about running away. All the time. Not any-more. Not after I'd forgotten to delete my internet search history and he saw I was looking at apartments in Seattle.

His threats to hunt me down and kill me if I ever tried to leave him terrified me to my marrow, but it was more than fear keeping me here.

My mom had loved this town with all her heart, especially during Christmas. Staying here, immersing myself in the magic of wintertime, was my way of being close to her. Besides, I couldn't give up on my dream.

When I was growing up, my parents owned an ornament shop called Kringle's. My dad had to sell it to pay for Mom's chemo when she'd gotten sick. The building was a cheesy gift shop now that catered to the tourists who came in for the Christmas season.

The building was big. I couldn't afford to buy it back, but I was able to buy the smaller one across the street. My dream was that one day, I'd make enough money with my business to buy back the old building to set up my shop. For now, I'd settled for the view of Kringle's across the street from my storefront window.

I closed up shop for the day, collecting my wreath and Bastion's present before leaving. I'd give almost anything to be able to stay in the shop all night. Hell, I'd gladly live in the little office at the back of my store if I could. But I'd stayed overnight exactly once. It hadn't even been on purpose. I'd accidentally fallen asleep in my chair one night, entering my daily sales into the accounting program. Hogan flew off the handle, accusing me of cheating on him. It hadn't mattered that I had footage from my security camera proving I'd been alone in my office all night.

The fucker had hit me anyway.

I climbed into my Subaru and watched the tourists and locals packing the streets, marveling at all the Christmas lights and beautiful storefront window displays. I opened my glove box and moved to shove Bastion's present inside. The compartment's little light bulb made the bow sparkle.

I doubted I'd get much of a present from Hogan. He said my engagement ring was so expensive that it was basically my present for the foreseeable future. Apart from the box of oranges my dad had sent in the mail, and the little gifts some of my regulars dropped off, I doubted I'd get much of anything this year. That made Bastion's gift exciting. What could it be?

Despite owning a Christmas tree farm, Bastion wasn't exactly big on the holiday. His parents were gone, too, and this time of year seemed hard on him. Not that he'd ever say that, but he wasn't the only one who could read between the lines.

I opened the package delicately, thinking I might make some cute paper bows out of the salvaged wrapping paper. Maybe I'd buy a present for him, something small if I could keep Hogan from finding out, and put the bow on it.

My throat tightened when I pulled out a book. It was a romance novel, a Christmas-themed one. I read the blurb, and the lump in my throat continued to swell. It was a spicy retelling of *The Nutcracker*.

I flipped through the book, and my breath latched in my chest when I noticed the inside cover had a note.

> Clara:
>
> I know you love books. Notice you reading them all the time. You always insisted on playing Clara in the school's Christmas play of *The Nutcracker* because your mom had named you after the main character. I'm sure you have a million copies around, so I thought I'd get you something a little different. I heard the heroine in this retelling is a badass. The rat king gets the girl, but he doesn't have to save her. Clara saves herself. Figure you'd like it.

I read the last couple of lines several times over before hugging the book to my chest.

*Clara saves herself.*

I sat in my car, staring down the darkened driveway that led to Hogan's farmhouse. Most nights, I'd park by the wooden sign reading *Hogan's Happy Hogs* in big red letters with a painted character of my fiancé dressed up in a Krampus costume.

I never sat at the end of the driveway for long. He knew the shop closed promptly at five, and while it took twenty-seven minutes to get to his farm from town using the main road, I'd found a shortcut that only took twenty. That bought me seven precious minutes to myself, which I used to mentally prepare myself for an evening with Hogan and his unpredictable temper.

My attention landed on the wreath in the passenger seat.

The handsome, annoyingly-observant, Christmas-hating Bastion had been right.

I tried to make everything as perfect as I could outside my horrible relationship. Staying laser-focused on the things I could control, making them exactly how I wanted, was a much-needed distraction.

I pulled out the wire twist ties I'd been keeping in the glove compartment, and my new book caught yet another long beat of my attention before I stepped out of the car and into the cold.

It had started to snow.

I smiled to myself, the first genuine smile I'd worn all day. My mom loved the snow.

For a blissful moment or two, I sat in the quiet snowfall, affixing my new wreath to the grill of my car until it was just right. I stood back to admire my handiwork, framed by the headlights of my car, when something shifting in the shadows snagged my attention from my task.

My eyes strained through the murky dark. I could have sworn I'd seen something shift. Maybe one of Hogan's hogs had gotten loose. Sometimes that happened. But something told me it wasn't that. I shrugged it off, deciding not to tell anyone. People saw shit out in these mountains all the time, and the entire town would write it off as a Krampus sighting every damn time.

It was stupid, considering this was Washington state. Bigfoot, maybe. But the Krampus? Even if monsters were real, the Krampus was supposed to frequent central Europe. Not the Cascade Mountains. Still, every "sighting" would pull in more tourists.

Nothing like a horned monster with a switch and the promise to punish the naughty to draw in the crowds. Sure, people came to Leavenworth for all the lights, the hot chocolate and the sledding. But regardless of the holidays, people were still perverts through and through.

A buzz in my jacket pocket drew my attention from the movement in the dark. My cell phone's screen lit up with a series of deranged text messages.

**Hogan**

Where in the fuck are you?

Are you with that fucking vendor?

"That vendor." This was a small town. Everyone knew every-one. And Hogan had known Bastion for years.

I saw you with him.

My chest filled with ice, and every breath I took turned painful. With shaking fingers, I tapped out my response.

Clara

He was just dropping off the last load of trees I ordered.

I know you didn't have a delivery today.

He saw I was out. He delivered early.

Every place in town is sold out. So why did he pick you, of all the places that sell trees, to deliver early? What favor does he owe you? And what in the fuck is he doing giving you a present?

It was just a book.

It was pointless trying to explain the situation. Hogan never listened. He'd jump to conclusions, and there'd be no convincing him otherwise.

Get the fuck home right now.

There was a part of me—a big part of me—that wanted to climb back in the car and drive as far away as I could. But Hogan was just insane enough to track me down. Just one more night, then I'd look into escaping him tomorrow.

Then again, that's what I always told myself.

Besides, what else was I supposed to do if I couldn't bring myself to abandon my shop and my dream to relocate into my mom's old building? This was a small town. No one was going to protect me from him. Even if everyone found out that the "Honied Ham Man" and the florist weren't such a perfect couple after all, it was doubtful they'd believe Hogan was capable of such brutality. He ensured never to leave a mark, at least not where anyone would see.

The town loved him. They didn't know the real man behind the mask.

These days that was the one thing we had in common. We were both great actors.

I pulled my Subaru into the driveway beside Hogan's work truck, steeling myself for another beat before walking through the front door of the house.

To outside eyes, the little yellow farmhouse was cute. The perfect home. Especially with the Christmas lights on the eves and the wreath—another one I'd languished over—hanging from the red-painted door.

I hated it. The inside smelled like old bacon grease, no matter how many times I scrubbed the place clean.

I set my purse on the kitchen counter and walked to the fridge, opening it. I tried not to flinch when the football game from the living room turned off, and the groaning springs of Hogan's old La-Z-Boy announced he was getting up.

Heavy footsteps drew closer. My breathing turned short and shallow with the monster's approach.

"Look at me, Clara."

I wanted to defy him, but I knew what would happen if I did.

Reluctantly, I glanced up from the fridge to find Hogan standing in the kitchen doorway. His large frame filled all of it. He used to be handsome before all the pork took its toll. In high school, he'd been every girl's—and some of the guys' too—crush, with curly blond hair and blue eyes. He was different now in every way.

My eyes dropped to the glass of whiskey in his hand. His drinking problem was to blame, but I didn't dare say that out loud.

I cleared my throat and donned one of my signature fake-as-fuck smiles. "What do you want for dinner?"

"No, you don't get to fucking do that."

"Do what?"

His flushed cheeks flamed an angry hue of red with his savage scowl. "Act like little miss innocent. Like you didn't do anything wrong."

"I *didn't* do anything wrong."

"Right. You lying bitch. You know, you're clever, I'll give you that. Everyone in town thinks you're so perfect. With your flower shop and your little woe-is-me story about your mom."

Something inside me flared to life, a rage that I usually suppressed for my own safety. But Hogan normally didn't bring up my mother. He wasn't a bright man, but he usually knew to stay away from that topic.

"What do you mean, my woe-is-me story? You mean my mom getting fucking cancer and dying just a few weeks before Christmas? Then how my dad up and left me not even a full two months later for some stranger he met on the internet?"

"Yeah. And it happened two years ago. Get the fuck over it. And when I say get over it, I don't mean by fucking that tree vendor of yours. If I catch him that close to you again, I'll kill you both."

# Chapter Three

## Clara

Hatred painted my vision red.

I wanted nothing more than to wrap my hands around this bastard's fat neck and squeeze until the light left his eyes.

Too bad Hogan Humpries was still built like a linebacker even though his high school football days were long gone. And his diet, which consisted of sixty percent honied ham, really had a way of packing on the extra pounds.

Meanwhile, I was five foot two inches, and he could snap me in half. When we'd first started dating in our junior year of school, the size difference had made me giddy. Now, it just made me sick, knowing I'd never be able to fight him off.

He'd never done more than hit me a few times, but there was a look in his eyes I'd never seen before. Hogan looked at me like I was nothing but a bug, and he wanted nothing more than to crush me beneath his boot.

Which was insane, considering I'd never cast more than a few lingering looks in Bastion's direction. This didn't have anything to do with jealousy, though. This was about Hogan doing anything within his power to feel bigger than the insignificant, chicken-shit man that he was.

"I'm not going to just *get over* my mother's death, you fucking asshole."

I wasn't exactly a stranger to tense domestic situations. Cussing out the man who just threatened to kill you wasn't exactly a wise move, yet I couldn't seem to make myself care. The typical surge of fear wasn't hitting like it usually did. It was like something inside me had finally snapped.

The only thing pumping through my veins now was visceral rage, wound tight with adrenaline. Then, cold, hard reality slammed into me. This wasn't the man I'd fallen for in high school. He'd turned into a violent drunk, and he wasn't coming back from that. If I didn't get away from this man, one day, he'd kill me. And if I left him, he'd kill me.

What else was there to do?

*Clara saves herself.*

Hogan struck me, his hand smacking my cheek so hard I saw stars, and my eyes swam with tears. I didn't allow them to fall as I composed myself. I refused to let him see me cry.

Instead, I forced another of my signature smiles. "I'm sorry. Please. Just let me make you dinner, baby. I'll make your favorite."

Hogan glared at me for several barbed seconds before turning to retreat back into the living room. "Fine. Bring me a drink while you're at it. Some of that boozy eggnog I like."

"Sure, babe."

I stood frozen in the middle of the kitchen until I heard the spring of Hogan settling back into his La-Z-Boy, and sounds of the football game filled the living room. I opened a drawer, pulled out my apron—with the words "Christmas Calories Don't Count" and a picture of a gingerbread man biting the head off another gingerbread man on it—and tied it around my waist.

Placing my phone on the counter, I flicked on some cheery Christmas music to drown out all the horrifying thoughts bouncing around in my brain. I smiled when "Carol of the Bells," my mom's favorite, came on.

"Turn that shit down!" Hogan roared from the living room. "We listen to that fucking trash all goddamn day."

I turned the volume down with a poisonous smile, the movement making my cheek sting.

Heading into the attached garage through the door in our kitchen, I went to the chest freezer shoved against the far wall in search of Hogan's favorite: ham steak.

When I pulled out the ham wrapped in white butcher paper and shut the lid, the utility shelf behind the freezer caught my eye. Dozens of plastic bottles—all various auto fluids and cleaning supplies—sat there, but a bright red bottle, in particular, struck a chord with me.

Antifreeze.

I stared at the bottle for what felt like forever as "Rockin' Around the Christmas Tree" played from my phone in the kitchen.

*Clara saves herself.*

The words from Bastion's note played in my head on a loop.

"Clara saves herself," I whispered under my breath as I reached for the antifreeze, tucking it in my apron pocket and retreating back to the kitchen with the ham I didn't intend to serve.

For the first time in a long time, I enjoyed making Hogan dinner. I knew by the time the night was over, he'd be dead. And I'd be free.

I unwrapped the ham steak in the sink and stood over it for a moment. It was like I'd finally unlocked the box at the back of my brain where I'd carefully tucked all my trauma away for the past two years and allowed it to spread through me like poison.

My hand slipped into my apron pocket, fingers teasing the lid of the antifreeze.

Dark images played in my head as I imagined Hogan's dead body slumped over in his La-Z-Boy... A cold smile curved my mouth.

If I went through with the dark thoughts whirling in my head, Hogan wouldn't have a chance to enjoy his ham. And after this nightmare was over—if I could escape it—I'd never eat ham again, even if there was a gun to my head.

"Where's my fucking eggnog?" Hogan's drunken roar pierced my murderous thoughts wrapped in cheery Christmas music.

The smile crystallized on my lips.

Whatever hesitation I had before was gone.

Tonight, I was going to kill the monster. Fuck Hogan. Fuck the consequences.

Even if I got caught, freeing myself of Hogan would be the best Christmas present ever.

"I'm making it now, babe! Just had to put the ham in the sink to defrost." I went to the fridge and pulled out the bottle of boozy eggnog to find it mostly empty. Of course. Hogan downed this shit like water. I went to the pantry and pulled out a fresh bottle among the stock I'd learned—the hard way—to always keep on hand.

I made him drinks every night, and just like every other night, I pulled a glass from the cupboard, poured the eggnog, and added an extra two shots of brandy, a sprinkle of cinnamon and an ice cube shaped like a candy cane.

The only thing new was the antifreeze I added to the glass. Hopefully, it would be enough to kill him. I'd watched enough TV and read enough dark books to know antifreeze didn't have much of a taste, and it didn't take much to kill a man. Making it the perfect poison.

The only thing was that it gave the drink a faint green hue. Hopefully, Hogan was too drunk to notice.

I walked into the living room, approaching my fiancé from where he sat in his chair beside the Christmas tree with that bright smile like I always did, playing the role of the good, obedient spouse he wanted me to play. Meanwhile, I imagined how he'd looked minutes from now, slumped over his chair, the light gone from his eyes.

My smile grew as I offered him the glass. "Here you go, babe. Made with love."

The hog farmer eyed the liquid inside, his ruddy nose wrinkling. "Why's it green?"

Fuck.

"Uh... I added some food coloring. Thought I'd make it more festive since Christmas is right around the corner."

I forced my hands steady, refusing to let my nerves give me away. A single bead of sweat slipped down my brow, but my smile stayed in place as "Last Christmas" carried from the kitchen, filling the tense silence.

Relief swept through me as he finally took the offered drink with a grunt.

I stood there, watching him take a sip with my breath latched in my throat. An eternity passed while I waited for his reaction. Would he notice something was off? If he so much as suspected that I'd tampered with his drink, he'd be the one doing the killing.

"Why are you standing around staring at me? You're like that fucking Bastion," he snarled after downing half the poison, cinnamon clinging to his upper lip. "Always staring like a fucking creep. Get the fuck back in the kitchen and make that ham, Clara."

"Sure, babe. Coming right up."

I practically skipped back to the kitchen. He hadn't detected anything was wrong. Now, to wait.

In an attempt to calm myself, I sat at the breakfast table and flipped through old pictures from past Christmases, back when my mom was alive and before Hogan had turned into a completely different person.

An older picture buried deep in my camera roll caught my attention, and I paused to admire it for the first time in what had to be years. I was sitting in my mom's lap beside the tree, giggling as I held up *Barbie and the Nutcracker* on VHS. I was seven at the time, and my only problem in the world was that I couldn't marry the Nutcracker from the movie. That was back when we still lived at the cabin my parents owned in the mountains.

I'd begged my dad not to sell it after Mom passed. It was old, and the one road leading to it through the pass often got snowed in, so Dad had put it in my name. I'd kept it a secret from Hogan, who thought that my dad had gone through with putting it on the market.

I still hadn't managed to get myself to go up there yet. Not when there were so many memories there. So many good Christmases. I still wasn't ready to deal with just how cold and empty it was now.

An angry, pain-laced scream followed by the crash of furniture had me leaping out of my chair, doing a sweep of the counter to make triple-sure that I'd hidden the bottle of antifreeze. On the next breath, Hogan stumbled into the kitchen.

"What did you do?"

If I hadn't just spiked his eggnog with a cup of antifreeze, I would have figured he was drunk. All the signs were the same. He was swaying like he could barely hold himself up. His face was bright red, his eyes bloodshot and filled with violence. His breathing was labored, and the veins in his brow looked fit to explode. Any moment, he'd pass out. Only this time, he wouldn't wake up.

It would be so easy to blame his death on alcohol poisoning. It wasn't exactly a secret that Hogan loved his booze. No one would question it. They especially wouldn't question his sweet, obedient fiancée and high school sweetheart.

I turned the faucet on, pretending to brush the frost off the ham like the good little wifey I could have been—If he hadn't turned into the monster he was today.

"I—I don't know what you're talking about, babe," I smiled sweetly before humming along to the Christmas music. "Are you alright? Having heartburn again?"

"This isn't heartburn, you stupid bitch." He was frothing at the mouth now.

Fear started to set in as I questioned the dosage of poison I'd given him. A cup should have been plenty.

"Babe, w—why don't you go lay down? You'll feel better in the morning."

He stumbled toward me, arms outstretched, a black sort of hatred in his eyes that told me if I let him get his hands around my throat, he wouldn't let go until I was dead.

"What did you put in my drink?"

My feet shuffled backward. "N—nothing! Just some food coloring. Everything else is your usual drink—"

"Stop lying, you fucking cunt! You put something in it!"

# Chapter Four

## Clara

Hogan's angry words came out slurred, almost indecipherable now if it weren't for the fact that I had lots of practice listening to his drunken tirades. His speech grew sloppier by the second, and as he lumbered toward me, he started to sway dangerously.

I didn't believe in shit like God. Sure, I was a big Christmas fanatic, but for sentimental reasons and because I associated it with a life I'd never get back. But at that moment, I prayed to God or whoever was listening that Hogan would drop dead before he could get his hands on me.

That look in my fiancé's eyes, the one that revealed all the ways he intended to hurt me, reminded me that even if God was real, he wasn't going to save me.

*Clara saves herself.*

Hogan lurched forward and made a swipe at me with his meaty arms. I shot to the other side of the kitchen and grabbed the large meat cleaver from the knife block.

Hogan snarled, flecks of antifreeze froth and saliva hanging from his chin in disgusting tendrils oozing all over his "Hogan's Happy Hogs" polo shirt. "Why are you fighting back? You should know by now how useless that is. I always win, *baby*. Know why?"

I glared daggers at him as he continued on his rant while the festive music played in the background, oblivious to the domestic nightmare.

"Y—you're not one of the chicks in those pervy lady books you're always reading. This isn't fantasy land, Clara. Come back to reality... Where..." he groaned as the poison seemed to take its toll on his body. "Where you're nothing."

My teeth clenched, my palms turned slick with sweat, and somewhere deep in my being, I felt a fire burst to life.

I swiped at him with the knife, and a scream jerked from his mouth as it caught him across the chest, a shallow cut running between his nipples. He stumbled back into the breakfast table, collapsing into the chairs. The furniture scraped against the linoleum as his huge form crashed to the floor.

Recognizing the precious few seconds I'd been given, I debated running. I still wasn't a murderer. I could run away and leave these mountains forever. But then my shop would be gone, along with the dream of buying the old Kringle building across the street. I'd lose my parents' old cabin. I wanted to go back to it one day, but I couldn't while Hogan was still alive, haunting this town like a drunken ghost of Christmas past.

If I left, I was sure I'd never see Bastion again.

I jumped on top of Hogan before he could get back to his feet, and with both hands on the hilt, I slammed the cleaver's deadly edge toward his throat.

He caught my wrists with a roar and, using all his strength—which was still a lot—threw me off him. My frame slammed into the cabinets beneath the sink, and the door sprung open with the force. The mostly empty antifreeze bottle tumbled onto the linoleum.

A terrifying expression warped Hogan's face. He knew that wasn't where he'd left the antifreeze. Before I could react, he was on top of me with his hands around my throat.

"You *poisoned* me?"

As his sausage fingers tightened around my throat, restricting my airflow, darkness crept in around my field of vision.

*Clara saves herself.* I kept repeating those words in my head like the lifeline they were.

This wasn't over yet. In Hogan's drunken, half-poisoned stupor, he seemed to have forgotten one important detail: I was still holding the cleaver.

I brought the blade down onto his nose, cleaving it in half. Blood gushed down his face, splattering my "Christmas Calories Don't Count" apron. He released me with a howl of pain, and I bolted to my feet, slipping on the blood that quickly began pooling on the ground before plucking my purse from the kitchen counter and scrambling outside into the snow.

I bolted to the car, my shaking hand plunging into my purse in a desperate search for my keys.

I hadn't looked back. I didn't know just how much I'd managed to hurt him, but Hogan Humphries was a tough bastard, and if he had so much as a shred of life left in him, he'd come out here and use it to rob me of mine.

My fingers closed around my keys, and a curse dropped from my lips, along with a puff of cold breath, as I unlocked my Subaru and flung myself inside the driver's seat.

I jammed the keys into the ignition. The engine sputtered to life, and my headlights bathed the garage door in a blinding white glow.

Hogan appeared on the porch of his house on the next pound of my heart. His face had a savage wound running from the bridge of his nose down to his lips, where the cleaver had split them in half. Blood dripped on the unshoveled walkway as he stumbled in front of my car, the bright drops of red staining the fresh snow.

It wasn't until he was in front of my car, with the headlights lighting him up like a grisly Christmas decoration, that I noticed the weapon in his hand. He'd grabbed the shotgun he usually kept mounted over the mantle.

"Oh *fuck...*" Unholy terror zipped up my spine as Hogan raised the shotgun and pointed it at the windshield. Then, clarity set in and the fear was gone as quickly as it had come. I knew what to do.

I shifted the car into drive and rammed the gas pedal. The wheels spun on the icy driveway before the car shot forward and slammed into Hogan—pinning him to the garage door with my bumper.

The gun dropped from his grip, and he sagged against the car's hood, sputtering blood.

I paused, allowing the staticy cover of *The Most Wonderful Time of the Year* to filter from the radio into the quiet of the car cab as I debated my options.

There was nothing stopping me from reversing and leaving. I could go right to the police station. Maybe there was a chance I could get away on the grounds of self-defense. Although, the odds seemed pretty damn slim.

My stomach flipped as I stared into Hogan's eyes. No. This bastard didn't deserve to live another day. If he did, he'd hunt me down and make me pay for this night.

Stealing my nerves, I reversed the car... only to shift it back into drive and ram into Hogan a second time. Then, a third. My head started to whirl from the impact of the car crashing into the garage door again and again. I didn't care.

I rammed the grill of my Subaru into my fiancé—my soon-to-be ex-fiancé—until he was nothing but a bloody mass stuck to the garage door.

Finally satisfied, I pulled the car back for a final time and cut the engine before climbing out to survey the gory scene. There was no doubt about it. Hogan Humphries was dead. His corpse was nothing but a pulverized mass of meat and bone slumped in the driveway.

My attention slid away from the fresh corpse to the front grill of my car.

There was something really wrong with me since the only grief I could seem to summon was for the poor little wreath I'd spent hours perfecting. The bow was stained with blood, the branches twisted, and little bits of flesh gunking up the pine needles.

Instead of freaking over the fact that I'd literally just *killed* a man with his brutalized corpse smeared over his garage door, all I could think about was fixing my precious wreath.

Untwisting the ties that held it to the grill, I tugged the wreath loose and went inside to fix it.

# Chapter Five

## Bastion

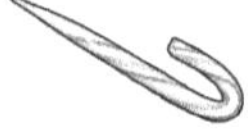

Hogan Humphries needed to be punished, and I was just the monster for the job.

I wasn't exactly the most experienced in the role I was born into. But just like my father and his father before him, it was in my blood.

I'd inherited a lot of things with my father's passing, like his struggling Christmas tree farm... which maybe wouldn't have been under such financial strain if he'd spent as much time managing his business as he did running around being what was basically Christmas Bigfoot with a penchant for justice.

While I didn't inherit my dad's obsession with being the Krampus, there was no escaping the dark magic that granted me the power to transform into a great horned beast with a serpent-like tongue, a horse-sized cock, and a wicked taste for retribution.

Unlike lycanthropy or vampirism, the monster disease was hereditary, and only one being at a time could carry it. So, four years ago, when my father passed away, I'd inherited the family business—held together by duct tape and holiday spirit—as well as the curse.

Lucky me.

My family was the reason our little town was known for Krampus sightings. It started when my great-grandfather migrated from Germany to these mountains around the turn of the century.

While it was Saint Nick's job to reward the good, it was our job to punish the naughty by shoving them into a sack, taking them into the mountains and beating them senseless. Then their memories would be wiped of the details and they'd be set loose.

*"You have the bloodline, Bastion,"* I remember my grandfather telling me when I was small. Too small to understand at the time that he was dying. *"One day, you will be the next Krampus. You will protect these mountains. Always remember, we don't kill. We're not that kind of monster."*

I was never interested in taking over my family's legacy, even though I carried the monster inside me. It wasn't like what had lived inside my grandfather. It was something dark and terrible, swirling beneath the surface.

I kept it locked inside me and never indulged those urges to punish and harm... Until I'd gotten the sense that the girl I'd been in love with since grade school was being abused by her piece of shit fiancé.

For the first time since my father's death, I was more than willing to release the monster if that's what it took to protect her.

I didn't have proof that the hog farmer was beating her. But as the Krampus, even when I wasn't shifted, I got feelings about this sort of thing. It didn't help that Clara was an expert at keeping her problems to herself. She didn't want anyone to help her. Ever since we were little, she'd always been insistent on figuring her own shit out.

If Hogan really was hurting her, she needed to get help or, at the very least, get herself to safety. Maybe she wasn't in a position where she could. So, I watched her like a hawk.

I didn't always follow her home, but tonight, something felt horribly off. My gut proved right yet again when she exploded from the front door in a blood-splattered apron. Moments later, after she got into her car, her fiancé stumbled after her with a shotgun clutched in his bloody hands.

Ancient, unholy rage filtered through my system.

For the first time, I felt my desire to indulge in my monstrous urges to their full extent. I wanted to take Hogan to the hidden mountain cave my family had used for years—stocked with chains and torture equipment. By the time I was done with him, he'd be a new man. Well, a dead one. But still new.

However, my evil plans disintegrated instantly once I registered Hogan's wounds.

*"Verdammter Scheiß,"* the German curse dropped from my lips with my next frozen breath. It looked like Clara had enough of his shit and was taking matters into her own hands…

What a good fucking girl. Naughty, of course. But damn, I was proud of her. What was more, seeing Hogan bleeding and frothing at the mouth—she must have poisoned him and probably took a knife to his face once the rotund fuck didn't go down—had my cock swelling in my pants.

That was the fiery Clara I knew and loved, the one she'd kept locked up tight for two miserable years.

I tensed from where I hid behind a giant blow-up snowman lawn ornament. I never shifted, yet I was ready to release the monster caged inside me at any moment to help Clara.

It seemed she'd taken the note I left in her Christmas present to heart. She was saving herself.

Clara jumped in her car and started up the engine. Hogan probably couldn't aim worth a shit, so he needed to get up close to take his shot… And he did, right in front of the car.

A deranged smile split my lips as I dug out a candy cane from my pocket and began to suck it into a point.

I had a feeling I was in for a show.

If Hogan weren't so sloshed from alcohol and whatever Clara had given him, I'd be on top of him in seconds, ripping out his throat with my claws. Regardless of the fact that Clara would see me shift in front of her. My secret would be out. Not that it mattered if that was the price for keeping her alive.

But Hogan could barely hold his gun up. His finger wasn't even on the trigger.

Clara drove the car forward, straight into her abuser and crushed the two-hundred-and-something-pound man into his garage door with her Subaru Outback.

She backed up, contemplating as he crumpled onto the frozen driveway.

Then she ran into him again, repeating the cycle at least half a dozen times.

My cock was painfully hard now as I watched the girl I loved reap the revenge I was sure she deserved.

The Subaru's tail lights flicked on, bathing the driveway in an ominous red glow one final time before she cut the engine and climbed out of the car. She walked around the hood as calm as a cucumber.

I thought she would start to clean up after her crime, but instead, she pulled off the wreath—the one she'd been trying to perfect at her shop today—and disappeared inside.

I stifled an incredulous laugh when she walked back out a few minutes later with all the gore cleaned off and a new fresh bow tied to the smushed branches and affixed it to her bloody and beaten car hood with a smile. As if the wreath fixed everything.

I couldn't help but stare in complete awe at this woman.

There wasn't much I cared about these days. The fucks I had to give were spread thin between being Krampus and running the tree farm, but my attention and ability to give a fuck never seemed to wane when it came to Clara.

Ever since we were little kids, I'd seen her for what she was. Full of fire and joy and a strength she didn't let anyone else see. And she smelled *so fucking good*. Like fresh ginger, clean linen, and coconut shampoo, although during the holidays, she switched to peppermint. I'd go into her shop right around the first of December just to smell it lacing the air, the scent stronger and sweeter than any of her floral arrangements.

I always knew she was tough, but this was a side of her I'd never seen before.

A new plan unfurled in my mind.

It wasn't Hogan who needed my punishment—Clara had that handled herself.

She was a murderer. She'd been well within her right to kill her fiancé... But I was the Krampus. It was in my nature to punish. With her, maybe I didn't need to keep the monster inside me locked up.

I knew what kind of books she liked to read. Whenever I saw her reading a new title between lulls at her shop, I went and picked up the book for myself.

Sweet, kind, level-headed Clara, who ran the darling little floral shop in an adorable Christmas town. No one but me knew what a little deviant she was. The kind that liked to be punished—in a certain way that a stupid man like Hogan Humphries didn't have the brain cells to understand.

I doubted she ever let Hogan read her books, not when it ran the risk of him thinking she liked his abuse. But I knew the nuances between the two.

Maybe there was a world where I could let the monster inside out to play, where Clara got her punishment for her crime and a reward for saving herself.

I could give her the kind of punishment she needed, the kind she'd love even as she screamed and squirmed.

My grin turned manic as I watched naughty little Clara begin to clean up her mess.

Hogan was gone.

Now, she'd have an even bigger monster to worry about.

# Chapter Six

## Clara

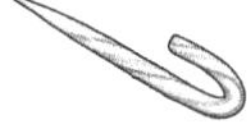

I was in deep reindeer shit.

The initial shock that rendered my system numb was wearing off. I'd *killed* someone. This went way beyond naughty list territory. I was going to prison if I didn't figure out how to cover up Hogan's murder.

Luckily, we were out in the middle of nowhere. Nobody was going to just happen across this, at least not tonight. I had time to clean up the crime scene. Although, after I'd bleached the shit out of the garage door and scrubbed away every last fleck of blood and gob of flesh, I was faced with the most difficult task of the coverup: hiding the body.

Hogan's crumpled form was still in my driveway, and I hadn't the slightest clue what I could do with it to ensure no one would ever find him again.

How was I supposed to get away with literal murder? Who the fuck did I think I was? One of the heroines in my books? *If only*. My mind went to one of my favorite heroines in a dark romance I'd read a while back. She had a stalker, and when she found out who it was, she fed his body to the hogs at a hog farm.

I gasped, realization piercing through me like an electric jolt. *She fed his body to the hogs.*

That was it! Hogs ate everything, even bones. Hogan's body could disappear without a trace, and even if people suspected the hogs ate him, it would probably be written off as an accident. He wouldn't be the first farmer to pass out in a pen filled with hungry pigs.

It was a perfect plan. Or, it would have been if I had the strength to move his body. Being hit by a car about ten times didn't seem to take any of the weight off. He was still heavy as fuck. There was no way I was dragging him to the barn.

I could get some chain and drag him with the car, but that would create a mess I'd never be able to clean.

I was trying to fend off crushing feelings of hopelessness when the crunch of heavy boots in the snow cut through the silence. Heart in my throat, I whirled around to see my Christmas tree vendor in the driveway with a candy cane clutched in his hand, his lips pursed around the sharpened point.

"Need a hand?"

My soul just about left my body, seeing Bastion standing there, *grinning* as I stood over Hogan's corpse.

A hundred questions flayed my mind as we stood there in complete silence for what felt like forever. Why was he here? Was he stalking me? How much had he seen? Was he going to call the cops? *And why was he fucking smiling?* Did he find this funny?

With every passing second, I was convinced this was all just a nightmare. This wasn't happening.

"No." I shook my head, trying in vain to swallow the lump in my throat. "You're not real. You're not here."

Bastion's bright blue eyes gleamed with amusement. "Aren't I?"

"No. This has to be a dream. I didn't kill my fiancé." My eyes stung with tears. For so long, I'd never allowed myself to cry around Hogan. But now that Bastion was here, they streamed freely down my cheeks.

"Well, if that's true, you have some pretty fucked dreams, Clara. But hey, I'm here for it."

"See, this has to be a dream. If this were real, you'd be calling the cops right now."

He canted his head, his dark hair falling over his ice-blue eyes in pieces. "Would I?"

"Yes, you would. Because if I get caught and you didn't report it, you'd be in a shit ton of trouble too."

"Well then..." He shrugged a shoulder and gave a tantalizing swirl of his tongue around the candy cane. "Don't get caught."

I blinked at him. Was he being for real right now? Was any of this for real?

My line of sight trailed back to Hogan's desecrated corpse. His blood had soaked into the ice and snow around him, creating a macabre snow angel that was all too real to be a figment of my imagination. And the relief that he was gone, combined with the adrenaline coursing through my system, was far too palpable to be part of a dream.

No, this was really happening.

I had killed my fiancé, and Bastion had seen me do it.

"What are you doing here?" I asked, apprehension prickling over my skin like needles.

"Going for a nice little walk, seeing all the Christmas lights."

What a fucking liar. We were miles away from town, let alone any other neighbors. He'd followed me here. I didn't ask him why. There was a more important question at hand.

"Are you going to call the cops?"

"I'm a lot of things, Clara, but I'm no rat," Bastion muttered, his eyes darkening as they settled on the corpse at my feet. The disdain carved into the lines of his handsome face had me seeing this man I'd known since we were little kids in a whole new light. "Not for Hogan fucking Humphries, anyway. If he pushed you to do this, the bastard had it coming. But this is serious shit. We have to get this cleaned up. *Now.*"

*We?*

"Y–you're going to help me?"

He sucked on his candy cane for a contemplative beat before answering, "I'll help you, but I need you to answer something for me. You have to tell the truth. If I sense for even a moment that you're lying, I walk away, and you have to clean up this mess on your own."

My anxiety lurched into overdrive, and I tensed. I didn't like people knowing anything about my life these days, but the reason for that was dead on the ground. The beans were spilled—the beans being Hogan's mutilated body.

"Fine. What do you want to know?"

Bastion's face hardened into a cold expression that turned my blood to ice. He'd never given me a reason to fear him other than worrying that Hogan would catch him hanging around at the shop. But somewhere deep in my animal brain, a little voice told me he was a predator.

Which was ridiculous. This was my Christmas tree guy.

Bastion strode toward me and nudged Hogan's smashed skull with a non-too-gentle prod of his steel-toed boot. "How long has this trash been hurting you, Clara?"

# Chapter Seven

## Bastion

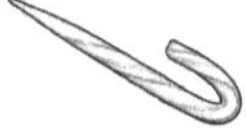

Thick tears poured down Clara's rosy cheeks. *Scheiße.* She was so pretty when she cried. I hadn't seen her shed tears since the second grade when Tommy Brown stole her Christmas candy on the playground.

"Is that why you've been stalking me lately? Because you thought you were protecting me?"

"That doesn't answer my question, Clara."

Her eyes flashed with anger. "You know what? Fuck you. Or however you say that in German."

"Fick dich."

"*Fick dich*, asshole." She swore at me in my first language and topped off the insult by flipping me off.

Clara was pretty when she cried, but she was even prettier when she stood up for herself.

It made my cock so goddamn hard.

She continued with her rant. She was angry, sure, but there was no missing the relief banked in her eyes. Like she was finally safe to let her true feelings out.

"You thought you were helping, but you just made everything worse. Hogan was pissed tonight because he thought I was cheating on him with you."

My brows furrowed. "How? We're never together."

"Yet you're always hanging around the shop for some reason. He thought you had me bent over my desk on the nights I worked late."

My cock ached again as I imagined it, but even as my dick thickened, something akin to guilt set it. "I'm sorry. I couldn't help but feel that you needed someone to watch your back."

"I don't need a bodyguard!" she snapped. "I can take care of myself. I can save myself."

I couldn't help but hope my inscription in the book I'd gifted her had inspired her to stand up to Hogan. Then again, she'd always had it in her. "You still haven't answered my question."

"I... A while, okay? I don't want to talk about it. Doesn't matter anymore anyway, the fucker is dead, and I have a body to hide. So, are you gonna help or not?"

A while.

The answer was vague, yet it told me everything I needed to know. Long enough that she didn't want to think about it. The couple had seemed happy before Clara's mom passed. Clara then focused on her dream of saving up money to buy her mom's old commercial building, and Hogan, being the needy baby he was, started to drink from the lack of his fiancé's attention. Then came the obvious shift in his personality. That was two years ago.

The knife of guilt sank deeper into my ribs. Had Clara been abused by Hogan for two whole years? Fuck. Why hadn't I figured it out sooner? I loved that she hadn't ended up needing me in the end, but I could have saved her so much pain if I'd noticed...

Maybe if I didn't focus so much on keeping the Krampus locked beneath my skin, my *knack* for sniffing out motherfuckers in need of punishment would be stronger.

My fists clenched at my sides, and another German curse barreled out with my frustrated snarl.

Clara took a step back, probably thinking I was angry at her. "You don't have to help me. I didn't answer your question. Just... Don't tell anyone. Please? I mean, if I end up in prison—" Her voice trembled and cracked. "That's fine. I deserve it. I mean, yes, he was trash, but I killed a man. A man with a family. A man who once, a long time ago, made me happy. But if this town is as magical as everyone says it is this time of year, and some bat-shit Christmas miracle comes true, I want to stay here in Leavenworth. With... With you."

Her confession had my cock blazing hot in my jeans while the ice around my heart seemed to melt some.

"I won't tell anyone, Clara." I stepped closer to her, and this time, she didn't step away. I reached out, brushing her cheek—her tear tracks now crusted with ice—and swept a lock of hair behind her ear. "Now. How are we doing this?"

She looked up at me with sparkly eyes, and the monster beneath my skin groaned, yearning to taste her.

It felt so fucking good to finally touch her.

"The hogs," she whispered. "They eat everything. Even bones."

"Then let's feed the hogs." I shoved the candy cane in my mouth with a toothy grin curling around the surgery shaft. "They're gonna eat good tonight."

I instructed her to grab a tarp from the garage to wrap his body up and then tossed it into the cart attached to the ATV Hogan drove around the farm.

Fortunately, according to Clara, he drove it to the barn all the time. So, any tracks left in the snow wouldn't be suspicious, especially if we left the ATV parked in front. As if he'd never gone back to the house.

Luckily, the cart already had a few empty beer cans inside. Conclusions would be drawn without much investigation.

"I'll get the body," I told her as I hopped off the ATV and crossed around to the back of the cart, bundling up the plastic-wrapped body in my arms.

"I'll help," she insisted, grabbing Hogan by his legs. "He's a heavy bastard."

I chuckled, knowing that I could easily carry both of them, one over each shoulder, even in my unshifted state. But I let her help as we shuffled into the barn, a symphony of oinking pigs excitedly greeting us, knowing a meal was on its way.

"Will they eat his clothing?"

"Hogs will eat just about anything," she grunted as we dumped the body into the pig pen and watched the beasts swarm their owner. "If they're hungry enough, and they are. Ever since Hogan started drinking, he's been pretty shitty about taking care of them. Especially during the holidays with his ham shop. He refused to hire extra help. Cheap jerk."

"Hogan's not so happy, hogs," I muttered as we watched them tear into their meal.

Casting a side-long glance at Clara, I was surprised to find a smile on her blood-splattered face.

I always thought I was the one with the monster locked inside. Turns out, Clara was also quite the little beast when pushed.

"I'm finally free," she sighed. "Ya know, on the off chance I get away with all this..."

"You will get away with it. You just have to be careful. We'll finish cleaning; then, in the morning, you can call the police and report that you fell asleep and Hogan never came back in from feeding the hogs. They'll come over and ask you a few questions.

No one will be surprised that he passed out drunk in the hog pen."

She chewed her plush lip with thought, and I couldn't help but think about what her perfect mouth would feel like against my flesh. Clara was fucking beautiful to the point where it was almost painful to look at her.

The monster inside me especially loved how she looked covered in blood.

I wasn't exactly a Christmas fanatic, but goddamn, did I love the color red. It especially looked good on her. Blushing cheeks. Blood-splattered lips.

Turning, I leaned against the fence so she wouldn't see the tent in my jeans. Watching her covered in gore, feeding her abusive ex to his pigs, was doing wicked things to me.

"Thank you for the book. I haven't even read it yet, but..." She turned to me, tears once again brimming her eyes. When her attention landed on me, her smile brightened, and the demon inside me paced impatiently.

"I guess I should go inside and clean up the mess in the kitchen."

She started to turn away from the pig pen, but I caught her by her coat. She paused to pin me with a look that had me stepping closer. Instead of pulling away like she always did when I got too close, she shuffled nearer to me.

I stroked my thumb over the edge of her jaw, marveling at how soft her flesh was. "Are you going to be okay?"

Clara peered up at me like I'd asked a silly question. Maybe it was. "How am I supposed to be okay after something like this? What am I supposed to do exactly? Sleep for a week? Drink myself stupid?"

She took a breath as if she was familiarizing herself with being honest about how she actually felt for the first time in years. "I don't want any of that shit."

"Then what do you want, Clara?"

She shook her head as if to dismiss the thought that came to her mind. "It's gonna make me sound crazy."

"I just fucking watched you murder the town's beloved Honied Ham Man and helped you feed his body to his hogs. Pretty sure that ship has sailed."

Despite all odds, she laughed. *Mein Gott.* The sound was heaven.

"Alright. You know what I want? To disappear into one of my books, literally. I want some dark romance hero to kidnap me and take me away from this place and give me the dicking of my life. And I know—" Her cheeks flushed, and her gaze flitted away, unable to hold eye contact. "I know it sounds crazy, fantasizing about being kidnapped after being stuck in an abusive relationship."

I gently gripped her chin and guided her attention back to me. "That's not crazy. You're allowed to fantasize about what you fucking want."

"I don't know..." she hedged. "You have no idea how twisted the books I read can get."

She hadn't the slightest idea that I read many of the same books I'd caught her entranced by at work. I knew exactly what kind of books she liked, what kind of deliciously depraved things she read about.

"I have an idea." I smirked. "The one I got you is a dark monster romance where the rat king gets the girl. I almost got you a Krampus one instead."

At that, she bounced on her heels in excitement. "I want to read that one too! I love Krampus. But not for the same reasons everyone else in this town likes him."

With a giggle, her cheeks flamed, and a new scent flooded the air—the candy-sweet scent of her arousal.

Clara liked the Krampus. No, she more than liked the Krampus. She was turned on by him.

That info went straight to my balls, and I had to bite back a hungry growl. "If only Krampus were real. Then he could be the one to kidnap you to the mountains. He punishes the naughty, after all."

The thick blonde lashes framing Clara's eyes fluttered, and the traces of her arousal spiked. Her attention slid to the feasting pigs, and something I parsed as shame etched her face. A barn filled with squealing hogs wasn't exactly a prime place for the dirty thoughts that were surely filling her pretty head. Especially considering what the pigs were eating.

I didn't care. Not wanting the moment to be over, I gave her an encouraging smirk. "What if it was the Krampus who kidnapped you to the mountains? Threw you in a cage? Made you his special pet.? Not for long... Just for Christmas."

"I'd..." Her face was on fire with a delicious hue of shame and lust, making my mouth water. "This is embarrassing to admit, but...I'd like it. I mean, I wouldn't want him to actually hurt me," she gushed, a combination of nerves and excitement making the words spill out of her like a faucet.

It had to feel great not having to watch what she said out of constant fear that Hogan was lurking around the corner.

"In my books, the heroes aren't usually *good* guys, but they'd burn the world down for their girl. So yeah. I guess if the Krampus was real and if he by some chance had that long tongue and a heart of gold? Then, yes. I'd let him stuff me in that sack of his and beat me with whatever stick he's packing. There, happy?" She huffed. "Now that you've watched me murder a man and confess my most embarrassing fantasy, you have all the dirt you could possibly want on Leavenworth's favorite florist."

Oh, I had so much more than dirt on her. Or, at least, I would soon.

"You should get some rest," I urged, eager to change the subject before I ripped off her clothes and fucked her here in the hog shed. "I'll finish the cleanup outside."

When she seemed hesitant, I added, "I'll do a very thorough job, Clara. I'm not exactly looking to get an accessory to murder conviction for Christmas this year."

She hesitated for another beat, then sighed. "Alright..."

I walked her to the front door of Hogan's farmhouse, and before going inside, she turned toward me, and her eyes darkened. "I would probably have gotten caught if it weren't for you helping to cover everything up. Thank you. I'll never forget this, Bastion."

Then, she pushed onto her tiptoes and pressed her lips to mine in a kiss I'd imagined a hundred times before. Her lips were soft and tasted of the medicated lip balm she used during the winter months to keep her lips from chapping.

When she pulled away, I fought the urge to tug her back into my arms and never let her go.

I shouldn't have said the words that were burning the tip of my tongue. Maybe it was the mischievous nature of the Krampus forcing them out. She had a way of drawing out the demon from where I kept him buried deep inside.

"Don't thank me, Clara." I licked my lips, lapping up lingering traces of her taste. "There will be a price for this."

# Chapter Eight

## Clara

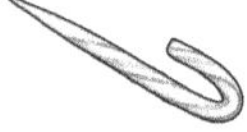

No matter how much medicine I took, I couldn't sleep. I tossed and turned until the early morning when the light started to pour in through the den's curtains. The tiny loveseat—at least three decades old and had belonged to Hogan's grandma—wasn't helping either. But I couldn't stand even the thought of sleeping in the bedroom or the living room. The den was the only place that didn't smell like my dead fiancé.

I flipped onto my side, trying to get comfortable even though I knew it was useless. The shallow sleep I did manage to catch, I dreamed of Hogan. But it wasn't just of the bad times. No, I dreamt of when we'd still been in love. When he'd been a completely different person. Back when we were still in school, naïve enough to think we'd always be together. Graduation. His proposal. Dreaming of our own business and saving together. Then it all turned sour.

Flashes of him choking the life out of me filled my mind, the cleaver coming down over his face, the sensation of his warm blood slipping down the handle and coating my shaking fingers. The hogs feasting on his ravaged corpse. Then the dreams shifted gears, and it was Bastion's face filling my unconscious thoughts.

I probably should have dated him in school instead, but all the kids were afraid of him—including me. Not because he was cruel but because there was always a dark, mischievous energy clinging to him that seemed to warn others to stay away.

I wish I hadn't.

His winter-cold eyes followed me in my dreams. Passing by my storefront window, always watching me. But I wasn't afraid. Not anymore.

Not even when he said those words to me after I'd kissed him.

*Don't thank me, Clara. There will be a price for this.*

What could he have meant by that?

Maybe it was a good thing he'd said that. It had pulled me out of the bliss that was our first kiss and brought me slamming back into reality. That kiss had been innocent and sweet—literally, his lips tasting like candy cane—but from that simple touch, I knew I wanted more of him. *Needed* more of him. I'd been about to invite him inside on some stupid pretense, like getting him to help me clean up the kitchen.

But then he'd said what he said, and I couldn't help but get sweeping chills that swallowed me whole, sinking to my marrow. It was that same demeanor he'd had ever since we were kids that scared everyone else off.

It only intrigued me.

Now that Hogan was gone, I could figure out the mystery that was Bastion Weber.

Finally, giving up on getting anything close to a decent night's sleep, I did as Bastion instructed, and I called the police to report Hogan missing. I was so anxious and scared that my voice shook, and Peggy, the dispatcher who I'd been in 4H with in middle school, assured me we'd find him.

When the two policemen arrived, also two people I was on a first-name basis with, they consoled me and told me we'd find him.

It was a good thing I'd kept mine and Hogan's problems a secret. Everyone thought we were still madly in love. There was no reason to suspect that I'd murder my high-school sweetheart and the love of my life. Not when I'd gone to crazy lengths to ensure my life seemed nothing short of magical. It had been a survival mechanism for me, but now that I'd murdered Hogan Humphries, it had its extra benefits.

The investigation wrapped up after a few hours. No conclusions were drawn, but I didn't miss the looks swapped between the police officers. They knew Hogan had been eaten by the hogs, and by the sympathetic pats on my shoulder and the invites to their houses to have Christmas dinner with their families, they didn't suspect me in the slightest.

The next few days were quiet. The only people who came into the flower shop were the occasional tourists, and the occasional looky-loo neighbor who'd heard the news and came in to give their sympathies.

Bastion had instructed me the night he'd helped me cover up the murder that I needed to lay low and not do anything out of the ordinary for a few days. I tried to read, and I couldn't focus on the words. I tried to make new arrangements, but they were uninspired and clearly lacked my interest.

I pulled out my phone and flipped to Bastion's contact. I'd saved him as "Tree Vendor" since Hogan went through my phone and got angry every time he saw a guy's name in my contacts. As if being on a first-name basis with a guy I'd known since elementary school made me a disloyal partner.

I stared at the number on the screen. Texting him wasn't out of the ordinary, not if it was about work.



I stared at the screen, waiting for the three little dots.

**Bastion**

No, Clara. You're well stocked. Checked this morning.

Why didn't you come in and say hi?

I'm busy. Planning a weekend getaway with someone.

With a heavy swallow, I stared blankly at the screen, reading the short text more times than I could count. A weekend getaway? Since when did Bastion go anywhere? I guess I wasn't involved in his life. I didn't know anything about his personal life other than that he lived alone and didn't socialize much outside of work. I'd just assumed he didn't get out much. The part of his text that stumped me most was the part about him going away with someone. Who? He didn't have family in the area anymore. As far as I knew, he wasn't seeing anyone.

Fuck. *Had I kissed a taken man?* No, Bastion couldn't have a girlfriend. He would have mentioned her. Even if he hadn't, I would have heard about it. This was a small town. People talked. A hermit like Bastion Weber having a romantic partner of any kind would be worthy of the front page of *The Gazette*.

This wasn't any of my business. I should have just put my phone down and got back to work. But I couldn't, not with this burning curiosity eating me alive.

> Oh? This weekend?

> Yes, Clara.

This weekend was Christmas. So whoever he was taking this weekend getaway with, it had to be someone special. Someone close.

> Who is this someone?

I tapped out my response and added a smiley face emoji to emphasize how nonchalant I was about it, even though my thumbs were practically sweating as I waited for his answer. Then I waited and waited some more.

The asshole left me on *READ*.

He didn't want to tell me, which confirmed my fear. This was a romantic getaway—it had to be. Otherwise, he would have told me who he was going with.

It didn't sit right with me how much this crawled under my skin.

I had zero business pining for my Christmas tree vendor when I'd only just got out of a relationship...and I was only single because I'd run over my last man. Why was I rushing to get involved with another? Hogan hadn't even been officially declared dead yet.

As if by some universal intervention, my phone rang. My heart sank when it wasn't Bastion's name on the screen but the Leavenworth Police Department.

Numbness spread through my body as I answered, and they proceeded to tell me that Hogan had been drinking the night of his disappearance and had passed out while feeding the hogs. The coroner offered me their condolences and invited me out to their place for the weekend since they didn't want me to be alone on Christmas. I politely declined their invitation and hung up.

The notion of spending Christmas alone didn't thrill me, but spending it with random townspeople didn't feel right. They didn't know me.

Bastion knew me.

He'd been the only one to notice something was off when Hogan was alive, the only one to check on me. When he'd suspected something was off, he'd followed me home, and when he saw me at my lowest moment, he'd helped me through it.

So, if I couldn't spend Christmas with the only person who seemed to give two reindeer shits about me these days, I'd spend it alone. But I couldn't go back to Hogan's farmhouse. Fuck that shit. No, it was finally time to go back to my parents' old cabin. Maybe I wouldn't be so alone after all, with the ghosts of

Christmases past from my childhood... and whatever else lurked in those mountains.

The rest of the week crawled by on its hands and knees.

I'd been sleeping in the shop since I hadn't been able to force myself to sleep at Hogan's. Luckily, some of the local farmers were helping feed the animals until the place was sold, which was a load off my conscience. I hated that farm, but what happened wasn't the hogs' fault.

I went back to the farm one last time to pack my things. There wasn't much, a few bags of clothes, boxes of books, cleaning supplies. When I drove away, I cast a glance in the rearview mirror and flipped off the "Hogan's Happy Hogs" sign with a terse smile as it shrunk into the distance.

The property would be Hogan's parent's problem now. They'd sell it, and I wouldn't see a penny since we weren't married, but I didn't care. I didn't need shit from that man, dead or alive.

Finally, the end of the week rolled around, and I closed the shop for the holidays, hanging a sign on the front door that read "Closed for the Holidays. Open Jan. 2nd."

I took a trip to the grocery store and then, with so much emotion burning like bile in the back of my throat, made the drive up to my parents' old cabin in the mountains.

The drive through the pass was dicey since the snowfall was heavy—thank fuck for all-wheel drive—but the driveway was clear thanks to the middle-aged couple who lived a quarter mile down the road. They'd lived there for years and had been friends with my parents back in the day. They even had a spare key and were kind enough to keep the pipes from freezing. When I'd texted them that I was moving back, they'd cleared the driveway with their snowplow.

I unlocked the door and stepped inside, a wave of nostalgia hitting me with the scent of old wood and dust.

I set the groceries on the counter beside a bottle of boozy eggnog—fortunately not the brand Hogan liked—and a note that said "Welcome home, Clare-Bear" with a little doodle of a bear holding an arrangement of poinsettias.

Tears welled in my eyes. Mrs. Birkmire had written the note, but in a way, it felt like it was from my mom. She'd always called me Clare-Bear.

I had a good sob over a glass of eggnog before cleaning the kitchen and putting the groceries away. Then, I pulled out the ingredients I'd brought to make cookies for the Birkmires to thank them for looking after the cabin while I was away.

Once the cookies were in the oven, I gave the cabin a light clean, knocking down cobwebs and sweeping away dust until it felt livable again. When all that was finished, it was time to fetch the Christmas tree I'd ratchet-strapped to the roof of the car.

The cabin was surrounded by trees, and I probably could have chopped one down myself, but I liked the idea of having one of Bastion's trees. Luckily, there'd been one left, like it was meant just for me. It was a little worse for wear, with sparse branches and a crooked tip, but as I set it up and topped it off with a few of my mom's old ornaments, I couldn't help but think it was perfect.

The oven beeped, and I pulled out the cookies, setting aside one of the gingerbread men for myself. I poured a glass of eggnog and settled on the couch with my snack and the book Bastion had gifted me.

The spicy retelling of *The Nutcracker* was quickly becoming one of my favorite dark romances to date. Of course, Clara was a full-grown adult in this version, and the rat king was the heartthrob.

I'd gotten to a particularly filthy part.

The rat king had used Clara as bait to lure the toy soldier into a trap. With the soldier captured, the rat king told Clara the only way to win the soldier's freedom was to make love to him while the toy soldier watched.

I'd always had a thing for monster romances, but this particular author had a way of getting me to question what I thought I knew about myself. A giant rat monster getting Clara off with his tail? It was kind of horrifying, and in a way, that just made it better.

As I read the *very* detailed sex scene, my breathing picked up, and a radiant heat settled between my thighs.

I hadn't had sex in well over a year. Hogan always got pissy about it, and sometimes he even threw shit when I refused to have sex with him. Eventually, he stopped asking. To say I was starved was a bit of an understatement.

Shimming my pants and panties off, my fingers slipped between my folds to find them completely soaked. I was so sensitive, the faintest touch to my clit had my spine arching off the couch cushions and my toes curling.

"Oh fuck…" The book slipped from my hand and fell to the floor. With my newly freed hand, I palmed my breast beneath my shirt, tugged at my nipple, and slipped a finger inside my dripping pussy.

My head fell back on the couch's armrest, and a breathy moan slithered up my throat when I sank a second finger inside me to chase the first.

I imagined I was the Clara in my book, wrapped up in the rat king's clutches, monstrous claws scraping the soft skin as he gripped my thighs, prying them apart only for his tail to slither between them. My thumb flicked my clit, pretending it was the tip of a monster's tail, teasing me before sliding inside my heat.

Movement in my periphery drew my eye to the window. I froze with my fingers still stuffed inside me, then relaxed again when I realized it was just the snowfall. No one was up here, especially not sneaking around peering through my windows in a blizzard.

Unless, of course, it was some kind of monster. I giggled at the thought as my fingers resumed their pace. If it were a monster lurking outside my window, I'd let them have a show.

# Chapter Nine

## Bastion

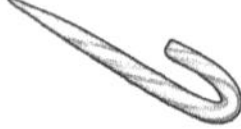

*Verdammter Scheiß.* It took every ounce of my willpower not to break down the cabin's front door and take her away to my cave right then and there.

I planned on kidnapping her; that much was set in stone since she'd revealed her secret fantasy to me. But not yet. My little beast was putting on such a tantalizing show for me, with her fingers stroking her perfect pink pussy.

She was even more beautiful than I'd imagined. Milky flesh and soft curves. Plush, fuckable lips on either end of her. When I finally shifted and pushed my long tongue between her legs, would her thighs tremble around my head? Would she grip my horns for purchase? Would she scream while her insides fluttered around my tongue?

My cock thickened in my pants as a hundred depraved thoughts whorled like a maelstrom in my brain.

I'd fantasized about this girl for years, and here she was, spread out on the couch, looking more perfect than I ever thought possible.

She was wearing nothing but a nightshirt, with her hardened nipples peaking against the thin fabric. The hand not currently occupied between her legs snaked beneath her shirt, exposing her midriff, and pinched one of her rosy buds between her thumb and forefinger, giving it a tweak.

"Fuck," she mouthed, her face twisting with pleasure.

The demon inside me clawed at my insides in an attempt to free itself. For generations, the demon had possessed the men in my family, driving its host to capture victims and feast on the suffering of the wicked. I'd suppressed its influence for years. Soon, I'd release it for the first time since inheriting the curse. But with this particular victim, the punishment would be different than what it was accustomed to.

I'd make her scream. I'd lock her up. I'd spank her and make her confess to her crimes, but I was going to make her love every depraved second of it.

Stalking her was nothing new. I'd been doing it for years, even before I'd gotten the feeling her relationship with the hog farmer wasn't all sunshine and roses like the rest of the town seemed to think.

Stealing a peek at her through her shop window, catching a hint of her scent and holding it in my lungs until my chest ached. Knowing when and where she ran her errands so I could schedule my tree and firewood deliveries around her day. I could always be there at a moment's notice because she didn't have anyone else in the world that gave a damn.

Watching over her was more than an addiction, more than an obsession. It was my goddamn lifeblood.

And now that I got to see her like this? Naked and worshipping herself beside one of my trees like a Yuletide goddess? It was enough to fill what the town called a "grinch" like me with the magic of the holiday.

The demon inside me flexed again, crying out for the mate it would soon claim, bringing an evil smirk to my lips.

Dark and despicable holiday magic.

My fingers dipped into my jeans and curled around my steel-hard shaft. The guilt of what I was doing quickly drowned beneath waves of pleasure, and I stroked myself with a frantic pace, chasing my release with monstrous abandon.

When Clara finally moaned her release and the shape of her lips formed my name, I came undone. With a strangled groan, thick ropes of cum coated my fingers and soaked into my boxers.

*"What a waste,"* I could practically hear the demon grumbling in my ear. *"Every drop of seed should be saved for my mate."*

My smile slipped, and in my post-nut clarity, I wondered how far Clara's thing for monsters and getting kidnapped stretched.

She loved those books, but that didn't mean she wanted those things to happen to her in real life.

It worried me, realizing as the demon inside me grew stronger, its vile urges more palpable, that it didn't care.

All it wanted was to sate its need to punish. *And what more of a perfect punishment could there be for the little beast than chaining her to my cock as my new mate?*

# Chapter Ten

## Clara

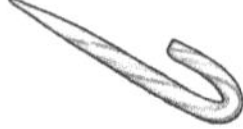

"Oh, fuck! *Bastion...*" I didn't mean to moan his name as I came. I blamed it on the eggnog, but it was more than that. Bastion Weber was more than just the town's enigma that seemed to cling to the shadows wherever I went. He'd inspired me to stand up to Hogan and helped me get away with literal murder.

His infuriatingly handsome smirk, wrapped around that candy cane he always had in his mouth, haunted my thoughts. I wanted him. There was something about him that called to my deepest desires. But now, when I was finally free to be with him, he'd ghosted me, leaving me high and dry.

I sat up, a surge of arousal leaking from my pussy. Okay, maybe not so dry.

My legs wobbled as I headed to the kitchen for another glass of eggnog and a cookie to drown my feelings, and another shift outside the window snagged my attention.

A chill shot down my spine as I padded to the window to find the figure of a man walking away from the cabin.

*Someone's out there.*

Maybe in a normal situation, if I was any other woman alone in a cabin miles away from civilization, fear would take hold. Hogan had been a piece of shit, but if he'd given me anything for Christmas, it was the gift of never fearing men again, knowing the deadly weapon I could be when provoked.

Wrenching on my pajama pants, oversized puffer coat and boots, I flew outside into the cold snow with nothing but the empty eggnog bottle clutched in my hand like a weapon.

The man turned, that smirk I knew all too well finding me through the snow. "And what are you planning on doing with that, little beast?"

"Bastion?" My insides twisted. "What the fuck? What are you doing here?"

It was the dead of night, in the middle of a blizzard. The driveway was mostly snowed in once again, and his car was nowhere in sight. "And how in Heat-Miser's Hell did you even get up here? The roads must be shit."

He shrugged with the nonchalance he might have had if I'd caught him on a casual evening stroll. "I'm German. I do well in this kind of weather."

I gaped at him with incredulous anger that seemed to be keeping me warm despite my lack of real pants. "Bastion. How did you know I was here?"

A million questions flew around in my mind, yet I knew the answer to that last question. He always had a knack for showing up in the same places as me. My shop. The post office. The grocery store. Even my house. But this? Showing up at a cabin I'd only just moved back into. No one but the Birkmires knew I was here. Even if he'd followed me from town, I'd been up here for hours.

"Were you watching me?"

The heated look on his face, with the twinge of shame, was the only answer I needed. I wanted to be angry, and I was...but the emotion was numbed by the surge of heat twisting through my body.

"I made a mistake," he admitted.

*Ugh.* He was so handsome, standing there with his jet-black hair flecked with snowflakes and his ice-blue eyes catching the glow from the Christmas tree lights shining through the living room window. Any other man who'd been standing out in the freezing cold for hours would be half-frozen, wet and miserable-looking.

But here he was, looking somehow refreshed by the cold. How was that even possible?

"A mistake. What mistake? You mean stalking me constantly?" The words wouldn't stop pouring out of my mouth. "Then ghosting me out of nowhere, making me think you're with someone else…only to find you lurking outside my window?"

His panty-obliterating smirk was gone in a blink, and in its place was something dark and predatory that I'd only seen brief glimpses of before.

"I watch over you, Clara," he growled, his voice laced with vindication. "I protect you."

"I don't need your protection, asshole. Clara saves herself, remember?" I stalked closer. "You still haven't told me why you're here. Because as perverted as you obviously are, I don't think you came all the way up here to watch me flick my bean. It's Christmas Eve. Aren't you supposed to be on a weekend getaway or some shit?"

"I was talking about *us*, Clara."

Was this guy for real? My brows furrowed into an angry V. "Oh, shoot. Sorry for not being able to read minds! You never said you were talking about me. You made it seem like you were with another woman. You let me sit here all night thinking you'd just up and ghosted me."

"I'm sorry, I was trying to surprise you."

"With what, a heart attack?"

The way he stared at me, with all the sadness in the world, had my heart aching. But there was something else banked in his icy eyes, too—something that had me feeling like I was staring at a dangerous animal through the bars of a cage. Watching and waiting, crouched at the ready in case I was foolish enough to get too close. And it was *that* look that had my pussy dripping all over again.

*Fuck*. I still wasn't wearing underwear. I pressed my thighs together to prevent fat tears of arousal from streaking down my thighs. A phantom smile tugged at the corner of Bastion's mouth. He seemed to know exactly what I was doing, but he had enough sense not to comment on it.

"It doesn't matter anymore. You need to stay away from me, Clara," Bastion said, shaking his head. "I'm not safe."

"What are you talking about? You've been following me around for years like the bodyguard I never asked for. Now, suddenly, you're the bad guy?"

"Yeah, that's right. I'm the bad guy. I'm like one of the monsters from your books."

I snorted. If that were the case, we'd be fucking right now.

"This thing I'm trying to save you from—you can't kill it. Not like you did with Hogan."

With a frustrated sigh, I pinched the bridge of my nose. All I wanted for Christmas was to understand this man. I shook my head, arms folding around myself to keep me from shivering.

"What *thing* are you talking about Bastion?"

"Something ancient..." Freshly fallen snow crunched beneath his boot as he took a cautious step toward me. "Something demonic."

"Demonic? Ancient? Wow, sounds like a good story you're cooking up there. Maybe you should quit tree farming and get into writing," I said dryly, finding myself wishing I'd brought my mug of eggnog outside to warm my stiff fingers. Any sane person would have gone inside by now to leave the psycho stalker out in the cold.

Maybe it was my curse to forever be drawn to this strange man.

He was magnetic, even when he looked at me like I was something to eat. Hell, especially then.

He took another step toward me and then another, slowly shrinking the distance between us. "Oh, I'm dead serious."

"Yeah? Fine, let's pretend for a second that I believe you. What ancient demon lives inside you, Bast? Or is this all just some metaphor?"

"No metaphor. A dark curse runs through my family, something my great-grandfather brought over when he immigrated from Germany. Something that runs in my blood. Something that allows me to turn into a monster."

"A monster? Like a werewolf?"

The corner of his mouth hiked up in a devilish smirk. "Like the Krampus, Clara."

Silence stretched between us as I waited for the punchline to drop. When none came, I laughed anyway. "Okay, *now* I'm being punked, right?" I did my classic gag of looking around for the hidden cameras. When I turned my attention back to Bastion, I jumped and clamped my hand over my mouth to stifle my yelp of surprise.

He'd devoured the several feet of distance between us without me noticing in under a second.

I peered around him to find there weren't any footprints from where he'd been to where we both stood now. As if he'd teleported.

"H–how did you do that?"

He produced another candy cane seemingly from mid-air and pushed the shaft into his mouth with that signature grin. "Magic."

Bastion always had this mischievous air about him despite the miasma of dark energy clinging to him, like the way he twirled the candy cane around his finger before sticking it in his mouth. His constant sweet tooth and his sarcastic jokes, paired with his white-hot gaze brimming with hunger, burned into my flesh like a brand.

The combination was fucking electric.

"Go back inside, Clara. You're shaking."

I *was* shaking, but it had nothing to do with the cold any-more.

He was so close we were nearly touching. My entire body burned with the need to feel his skin against mine.

Like something chemical going off in my brain, drawing me closer.

This time, I took the last step forward—my chest now flush with his, my palms smoothing over his pectorals. Even over his jacket, I could feel how built he was. Lugging lumber all day really kept him fit.

"You shouldn't be rewarded for spying on me, but I'm not going to leave you out in the cold to freeze."

He smiled as if I'd said something funny. "I won't freeze. My demon keeps me warm."

"What other tricks can your demon do?"

"You don't believe me. You think I'm joking." He lifted a finger to trail along my jawline, sending a shiver vibrating down my spine.

"That or you really believe you're the Krampus, and I just think you're crazy. But so what? I made you an accessory to murder. Who am I to judge?"

He gripped my jaw, his thumb rubbing my lower lip with a growling sigh. "If you invite me inside, understand what you're signing up for."

"Let's say I'm just crazy enough to believe you. I'm not afraid of you."

"Maybe you should be."

My chest clenched at his words, the frigid air sticking in my lungs. "If you're so dangerous, why have you been following me around? Why did you let me kiss you the other night?"

"I had no idea just how much my demon craves you until now."

A flutter erupted between my thighs at the way his eyes lit up, but I stuffed down the feeling, steeling my nerves. "I've faced bigger monsters than you. What are you gonna do, stuff me in a bag? Take me into the mountains and beat me with a stick?"

He licked his lips, that evil gleam in his eyes growing brighter by the second until his irises were glowing with supernatural incandescence.

"That's exactly what I'm going to do, Clara."

# Chapter Eleven

## Clara

After ghosting me and creeping on me through the window—though there was a small part of me that secretly liked the latter—I *should* have turned him out into the cold.

But the way he was looking at me had me buzzing with a lust I'd never felt with Hogan. It was a feral kind of need I didn't even know was possible to experience outside of books.

Even if he was full of shit about being the Krampus, which he was—because in what world could that be real life—it was hard to say no to that look. The one that promised all kinds of twisted pleasures and magical secrets.

How could I say no to that?

"How perfect. All I want for Christmas is to live out my dark fantasy of being kidnapped and dicked down in the mountains. The Krampus cock is a new element, but, hey, I'm flexible with the details."

I went back inside and held the door open for him. "Come inside. Unless you're kidnapping me right now, in which case I should probably put on real pants. Or maybe your dance card is full. *Krampusnacht* is over, but there are still plenty of naughty people to punish. Children to terrorize."

Kicking my boots off, I went to the kitchen to fetch the eggnog, forgoing the glass this time and flopping on the living room couch. Bastion slowly followed but didn't sit down. He stared at the tree, admiring all the antique glass ornaments and bubble lights.

"You're playing with fire. You think you're calling my bluff, but there's no bluff to call." He paused to admire one of the more modern ornaments, a faded paper Santa Claus I'd made when I was in the first grade. "Anyway, the Krampus doesn't punish children. At least, he hasn't for a long time. I think someone in my line at some point hated kids, so that's probably where that came from."

"So, the part of the story where the Krampus accompanies Saint Nicolas to punish all the naughty kids while Santa rewards all the good ones isn't true?"

"No, Saint Nicolas isn't real, Clara. Or at least not how society interprets him today. There's no *Krampusnacht,* either.

Krampus terrorizes whatever day he feels like, not just December fifth."

"So, what is real then?" I sat cross-legged on the couch with the bottle of eggnog clutched in my hands, happy for the company and the entertainment, even if I wasn't buying his story. Sure, he'd moved fast outside, and for a moment, his eyes seemed like they were glowing. I blamed it on the rum and brandy-spiked eggnog. "How do you figure out who needs punishing? Do you work locally? Are there more of you? How do you run your tree farm and still have time for this secret life? Are you like Bigfoot if he was Batman?"

"I love that you feel open to running your mouth now that Hogan's gone."

"I'm not running my mouth," I lied, knowing full well I was being a bit overzealous with my line of questioning. He was right, though. I did feel open to speak whatever was on my mind. It was refreshing. And even though he said I wasn't safe with him, being curled up on the couch talking about the Krampus in my old house with the man who'd helped me win all this back, I'd never felt safer.

"You are. And I like it." He prowled toward me, leaning down until he loomed over me with his hands braced on either side of the couch, caging me between his arms. His eyes were glowing again, their brand-hot heat making my skin explode with goosebumps. "But the demon might not find it so cute."

I knew this time that it wasn't a trick of the Christmas lights catching in his eyes or the spiked eggnog. His eyes really were glowing. My mouth dropped into an O as I gaped up at the man in awe. "How are you doing that?"

"Come on, little beast." That new nickname he had for me, *oof*. It was all gravely and wrapped up in all sorts of dark promises. "Don't you see the monster inside me? Can't you feel its need to hurt you? Doesn't that scare you?"

I could see the monster inside him, and I did feel its need to hurt me...

Though, now that I was slowly starting to believe his story—as insane as it was—I still couldn't summon so much as a lick of fear. Chances were pretty low that whatever possessed my tree vendor was anything like my ex. His promises of pain only had the place between my thighs growing slicker, hotter.

I was about to open my mouth and tell him once again that I wasn't afraid, but the words never left my lips. One of his hands lifted from the back of the couch and dropped toward my lap. His eyes stayed anchored to mine as his fingers dropped to the drawstring waistband of my pajama pants.

If I'd known he was coming, I would have worn something other than the pajama pants that said "on the naughty list." Felt a bit too on the nose now.

His fingers hooked into my pajamas, but he paused, and I realized he was waiting for my permission. I gave him the tiniest of nods, thrills of excitement making me squirm beneath him as his hand dipped inside my pants.

My head fell onto the back of the couch with a breathy moan as he swept his index finger over my labia. He chuckled, his glowing eyes sweeping over my face and drinking in the way it contorted with pleasure.

"*Scheiße*, little beast. All this talk of demons has you dripping."

My breath hitched as the pad of his finger swirled slow and tantalizing circles around my clit.

Slowly, he dropped to his knees on the floor in front of me as if in unholy prayer. With the way he was positioned, with the Christmas tree at his back, his face was cast in shadows, and his glowing eyes burned into me from the darkness.

"Talking about demons is fun, but I think fucking them sounds like an even better way to pass the time," I said.

Bastion's finger changed up the pattern and paced around my clit, leaving me breathless as he considered my words for a tense moment.

"If I show you my other form, even just a small part of it, there's no going back. You can't unsee it. I have the ability to wipe your memories, but..." His smirk curved into a wild grin that seemed all too fitting for a man claiming to be the Krampus. "But I won't. I want my secret to torture you. I want the memory of what I'm about to do to you to keep you up at night. And when you do manage to sleep, I want it to slip into your nightmares, so I'm the only monster in your head."

Fuck me. How was I supposed to respond to that? All my ability to articulate was gone, and all I could manage was a sloppy nod. My legs parted, a silent invitation that I was not only into this, but I wanted more—*needed* more.

What we were doing, what we were about to do, felt wrong. Which, given my newfound freedom, felt so fucking right.

In a way, it was almost like Hogan was still alive, running his honied ham stand, wondering if I was off cheating on him with my Christmas tree guy. I could only hope that he was looking up at me from Hell, helpless to do anything but watch.

The fact that Bastion was literally some dark creature made for terrorizing people—which explained the strange aura he'd had since we were kids—only made this whole scenario that much more tantalizing.

Did he have horns? That *long* tongue? Did he wear chains? Would he use them for my "punishment?" Oh my God, did he have *hooves?*

If Bastion were really what he said he was, that would have been enough for any sane person to run for the hills. Not me. I'd read one too many monster romance novels and thought *fuck, I wish that were me.*

Now, it finally could be. Talk about one fucked Christmas miracle.

"I have an idea." Bastion's eyes glinted in the light. "A little game we can play."

"A game? *Oh!*" I gulped down a sharp breath as he pushed a finger inside me.

"I start showing pieces of my demon. Slowly. I let you see them—*feel* them. If at any point you fail to convince me you're having a good time, I leave. We keep each other's secrets, and we go about our lives pretending we fit in with everyone else."

"And if I prove what an eager little beast I can be for the alleged Krampus?"

His eyes lit up. "Then I make your darkest fantasy come true. The one you told me about on our first date."

I blinked. "First date?"

"Yes. When we fed your fiancé to the pigs, I count that as our first date."

"You suck," I told him, through an ear-to-ear smile that he matched with one of his own.

"You have no fucking idea." He sat back on his heels, pulling his finger from my pussy and bringing it to his lips to make a hushing motion. His lips parted, and his tongue wound around the digit to lap up my juices. The appendage was thick, oozing strings of saliva. It wrapped around his finger once...twice. It kept going. His muffled cackle scraped over my skin like sandpaper, leaving me pink and raw as I gaped stupidly at what was the longest tongue I'd ever seen.

That tongue could only belong to a demon.

# Chapter Twelve

## Bastion

I wasn't used to shifting in portions like this. Not that I was used to shifting at all. But this was good. I needed to take it slow and steady and show her what she was in for.

Given her past, I needed to be gentle... At least, up until she proved this was really what she wanted and understood what was about to happen to her.

Once I fully shifted, it would be the demon in control. Then all bets would be off, and Clara would be at the mercy of the Krampus.

At least, this way, I'd rest easy knowing I'd given her the chance to change her mind more than once.

Her eyes practically popped out of her head as she watched my devil's tongue snake out, winding around my finger to demonstrate its impressive length.

Her arousal seeped into my taste buds, making the demon jerk, and a mangled growl vibrated up my throat.

"You taste like heaven. Funny flavor for such a slutty little beast."

Oh, she *liked* that. The tell-tale scent of her need laced the air, winding tight with the aroma of fresh gingerbread and pine needles. She squirmed, and I might have missed the beads of arousal leaking from her pretty pink cunt if it weren't for the tracks they left behind, glistening in the Christmas lights.

I wasn't one for Christmas but fuck, I could get used to this.

Gratification sizzled through my veins at the way her cheeks flamed, watching my tongue wind around the slender appendage.

"Holy fuck…" she muttered in disbelief as my tongue split at the end, demonstrating how it could separate in half. The hue of her cheeks went from pink to red. She was probably imagining how it'd feel splitting inside her. How it could stretch her like no other male's tongue could.

"What are you going to do with that?" she asked, her lashes all a flutter.

My tongue snaked back into my mouth, and I chuckled at the dejected look on her face. "What would you like me to do with it?"

She gave a little wiggle of her hips, and her eyes dropped to her center, making it clear exactly what she wanted me to do with my tongue.

I shook my head, letting loose an evil chuckle that had her writhing again—now in frustration. "No, you're going to use your words, little beast."

"I—I want you to tongue fuck me."

She was so quiet, speaking in barely more than a whisper. "Louder, Clara."

"I want you to tongue fuck me, dammit!"

As frustrated as she acted, I knew she was lapping up every second. And I loved watching her grow more confident speaking her mind, especially in this context.

My fingers slipped into the waistband of her pajama bottoms, and she instinctively lifted her hips, allowing me to slide them off. I gripped the undersides of her thighs and gently pulled her apart, loving the way she heated from her pussy to her cheeks as I examined her dripping cunt up close.

"Such a fucking perfect pussy," I groaned, deep and throaty.

I couldn't wait a second longer. I crouched between the cradle of her spread legs and snaked the tip of my tongue past her folds. A warbled moan wrenched from my lips the instant I pressed inside her. Her inner walls clamped around me, welcoming every slow inch that I fed into her with a fluttering kind of motion. I nearly came in my pants from the thought of her doing that to my cock.

Clara wriggled and moaned as I slowly filled her, delving deeper inside her until I hit her limits. I flexed and separated the severed muscle, stretching her and running the twin tips in alternating patterns. Her eyes widened, and she jerked against me, but I held her steady against the couch.

She babbled her pleasure, the sensation of the split tongue making a string of drool leak from the corner of her mouth. "S–so good."

Once she grew accustomed to the stretch, I began pumping in and out of her while keeping up the pattern with my tongue tips. She sobbed in ecstasy when I hit a particularly tender spot inside her.

I'd taken to calling her little beast because that's what she was—that's what I'd seen the night I watched her murder Hogan. But right now, she looked like a goddamn angel, shaking around my demon tongue. This was the kind of angel I wanted to mount at the top of my Christmas tree.

Her hands flew to my hair, and I peaked at her through the strands falling in my eyes, laughing against her pussy as she struggled to hold on. What she needed was handlebars.

A sharp pain shot through my skull but faded in a breath. A pair of thick horns sprouted from the top of my skull, black and ridged with a single spiral. Deadly tipped and pointed toward the heavens.

Luckily, I didn't need to pull my tongue from her so I could instruct her on what to do. She latched onto the horns, holding on for dear life as I probed and prodded, licking and lapping like a fucking wild animal who hadn't eaten in weeks.

I dragged my nails down her skin, allowing them to lengthen into claws.

The demon still hadn't taken over. It wasn't too late to go back. But the more I eased her into introductions with my other side, the more it became clear she wouldn't be changing her mind.

I chuckled. *So little miss monster fucker could put her money where her mouth was, after all.*

I was drunk on the pleasure of watching her buck against my hold, trying to push more of me in her. What a greedy little angel.

My rhythm picked up, and I tongue fucked her until she was screaming her release. Her core grew molten hot and wet around me, her heartbeat pounding against my tongue.

She went limp around me with a sated sigh. "That was fucking amazing."

It was cute how she thought we were done. We were just getting started.

I slipped out of her mound and gave her a minute to recover before the split head of my tongue found her clit, rubbing on both sides of the sensitive bud. Her spine arched off the couch, and her eyes rolled into the back of her head.

"It's too much…" I paused, and she gave a drunken shake of her head. "Don't stop. I'm winning this damn game. I'm getting my Christmas present, dammit."

If she'd allow a behemoth demon tongue to fuck her while my claws dragged vicious welts into her thighs, maybe she was ready for her punishment after all. How lucky for me that the dark creature inside me would be able to indulge its need for vengeance while the girl I loved fulfilled her darkest fantasy.

Talk about a win-win.

I filled her with a finger—making sure to retract my claw—and flicked her clit until she came again with another scream, this one more ragged than the first.

She sagged on the couch, her limbs like rubber, pieces of her blonde hair sticking to her sweat-moistened brow. The sight had my lips spreading.

I sat back, purring as she pinned me with a thunderstruck look. Her chest heaved as she caught her breath.

"Congratulations. You win our little game. Maybe you can handle the demon after all."

Pushing to my feet, I started to strip. First, I peeled off my shirt. Then I shed my pants. I stood there in my boxers and grinned at the way she gaped in awe at my chiseled body.

Finally, I shed the last piece of my clothing, and my cock sprang free.

I was still in my human form, but Clara regarded my cock like it was something monstrous straight out of her books. I was big, but she hadn't seen anything yet.

I couldn't hold back the monster any longer.

Black fur sprouted from my pores, covering much of my body. I grew taller until my horns scraped against the cabin's ceiling. Even the hair on my head grew longer until it fell in pieces around my broad shoulders.

The legs were the most painful part. They bent backward into haunches, tipped with great black hooves.

Of all my demonic features, my cock was what Clara's eyes clamped on to. It was thick and heavy enough that even rock hard, it couldn't stand up like it could in my human form. Ridges ran along the shaft in a spiral pattern, not unlike the striped candy canes I was always sucking on, stretching from my balls all the way to my mushroom head.

And it was seeing just how large I was and knowing what I was going to do with it that had Clara passing out on the couch.

I admired her beauty for several quiet minutes before gently scooping her up in my arms.

"That was your reward for doing whatever it took to free yourself from Hogan," I purred, watching her eyes flutter as my hot breath fanned her face. "Now for your punishment, little beast."

# Chapter Thirteen

## Clara

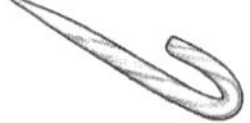

The last thing I remembered was swirling horns, fur as dark as rot, and those brand-like eyes burning a hole straight through me.

Bastion's demon flitted through my unconscious thoughts, haunting my restless sleep. The moment I woke up, I was convinced it had all been a dream. From feeding Hogan to his hogs to Bastion crouching between my spread legs and fucking me with his split monster-tongue.

Reality slammed into me when I realized I wasn't in my cabin anymore, cold dread crawling up my spine. I was in a cave, lying on a packed dirt floor.

I bolted into a sitting position, all the color draining from my face when I registered the metallic bars surrounding me.

I was in a cage.

Naked.

In what looked like a cave.

Those details almost didn't seem real. I had to repeat them in my mind until they finally sank in. I was in a cage, buck-ass naked, in a cave.

Another detail came zipping back to the forefront of my mind. Bastion, the weird kid that I had known since elementary school—and lately, my stalker and accomplice to murder—also happened to be a monster. Not just any monster, the half-goat, half-demon Krampus who punished the naughty.

Murdering Hogan Humphries definitely landed me on that list.

Bastion had done what he promised. If I "won" our game back at the cabin and could handle all his little demon traits, he'd let his full form out to play.

Luckily, he didn't count my passing out as a mark against me. Otherwise, he wouldn't have dragged me here.

Anyone else in my position would have woken up screaming. Not me. I woke up wet. Fucking. Dripping.

Bastion had not only helped me cover up Hogan's murder, but he'd revealed to me a secret of his own. Now he was helping me live out two fantasies: get kidnapped and be fucked by a monster cock.

A really, *really* big monster cock.

I was not a fainter, yet I'd passed out when I found myself face-to-face with the thing. I'd be lucky if trying to take that mammoth dick didn't kill me. What a way to go, though.

Shadows shifting at the edge of my vision had me looking up.

There he was. Bastion—no, the Krampus—lumbering toward me with something clutched in his claws. It was hard to tell what it was due to the long fur hanging from his arm.

"Looks like my little beast is awake. Merry Christmas."

The demon's voice was rough and guttural, making me shiver in delight. Its laugh upon seeing my reaction had just as visceral an effect on my body.

*It was Christmas.* That means I'd slept through the night...

I scanned the world beyond my cage. The cave we were in was huge and surprisingly well-lit despite the cave's entrance being nowhere in sight. That was thanks to the modern recessed lighting mounted into the rock walls. The place had been well-loved, as it was clean—for a cave—though it clearly hadn't been used in years.

"What is this place?" My gaze bounced between my surroundings and the demon.

"The Krampus cave. Tucked away high in the mountains where no one will hear your screams."

"I— Is this the place your father brought his victims to torture?"

The Krampus grunted in what I assumed was a yes.

"I figured there'd be more..." I did another sweep of the cave, looking for anything that might lend to the fact that decades' worth of naughty people had been brought here over so many past Christmases. But there was only a cage. Plus, the modern lighting really took away the creepy edge the place would otherwise have. "Torture stuff," I finished.

"Disappointed?" Another laugh, monstrous and so distinctly evil it had the hairs on the back of my neck raising. But clearly, none of this was a deal breaker yet because I was wetter than ever.

And thanks to my lack of pants, I was dripping onto the dirt floor beneath me.

The demon's nostrils twitched as he inhaled. His tongue—oh God, *that tongue*—flicked out, tasting the air. "Spread your legs for me, little beast."

I did as he ordered, even as an exciting cocktail of shame and excitement set my entire body on fire, my skin flushing a festive shade of red. My legs parted to reveal the wet spot I'd left in the dirt.

"Aw," the demon tutted in mock disapproval. He prowled closer, his hooved feet leaving strange prints in the dirt behind him. "Look at the mess my new pet has made all over my floor. That's okay, little beast. You're about to make a much bigger one for me."

I blinked up at my captor through the bars, my pussy fluttering as his menacing eyes drank me in. I was so turned on by all this.

Bastion warned me. He'd given me a lot of chances to change my mind about reenacting my fantasy. And fuck, I was so…*happy* that I hadn't turned back.

I was eating up every moment, my pussy practically on fire with anticipation.

I knew I was into some freaky shit, but I'd never had a chance to fully explore that with Hogan. Hell, I hadn't had a chance to explore much of anything with that bastard.

Bastion offered me a safe space—or at least what I knew deep down was a safe space, aside from all the bars and the terrifying demon looming over me—to let go of my inhibitions. To let go of control and just enjoy feeling owned. I could enjoy the faux fear, knowing true fear would never touch me again.

Anyone else would have probably told me to seek therapy. Bastion, on the other hand, whether he was helping me feed my abuser's mangled corpse to the pigs or throwing me in a cage on Christmas morning to "punish" me, was my therapy.

The demon prowled toward my cage and threw what he'd been holding inside. It clanked against the packed dirt in front of me, rolling to a stop a few inches away. I stared at where it landed in front of me, uncertainty bubbling in my chest.

It was an empty eggnog bottle.

What was I supposed to do with this?

Sensing the question perched on my lips, the monster leaned forward, pressing his gray face against the cage bars. His tongue wound around one of the bars, cackling. "You're going to fuck it for me, little beast."

For a moment, my brain stalled out. He wanted me to...*fuck the bottle?*

Tentatively, I picked it up and examined it. The cap was missing, and the liquid was pretty much gone, thanks to the little party I'd thrown myself last night. Only a few drops remained.

Jesus Christ.

Okay, so fucking a bottle seemed vanilla compared to the prospect of fucking what was literally the Krampus, but it wasn't just the act of inserting something that wasn't meant to be put in such places that had my nerves lighting up like a Christmas tree.

It was the thought of doing it locked in a cage while the demon watched.

"Do what I tell you, Clara," the beast rumbled. He held out his claw-tipped hand, and out of thin air, a switch appeared. He smacked it against the cage bars, making me jump. "You'll find I don't need to have my cave well-stocked with anything but you and me because I can make anything I want with magic..."

His switch disappeared, and in its place was a heavy chain, the links jingling in a way that was deliciously terrifying. "All I need is your naked body, little beast. Everything else is just a matter of being creative."

With a savage claw, he pointed to the bottle in my hand. "Now fuck the bottle, Clara. I won't tell you again."

# Chapter Fourteen

## Clara

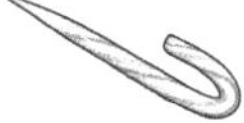

The bottle was so huge that I struggled to get a proper hold on it. I had to hold it with both hands. The Krampus cackled, his glowing ice-white eyes flickering as he lounged against my cage bars, enjoying the show.

"How are you going to take the Krampus' cock if you can't even take that bottle? Be the naughty slut you are, and show me how well you can hold your eggnog, little beast."

Oh God, his words were like gas on a flame.

I pushed as much of the bottle's neck inside my pussy as I could while gripping the bottle's base so hard my fingers shook.

"There we go, that's more like it." He licked his lips, his impossibly long tongue oozing with so much fucking saliva it seemed impossible that a single creature could produce that much fluid.

Probably sensing just how much I loved that tongue and all the spit it produced, his tongue slithered through the bars and wiggled above me, fat drops of saliva dropping to pepper my tits. The monster fluid coated my flesh, making me glisten beneath the cave's lighting.

I felt every bit like the naughty girl I was, writhing in a cage, fucking myself with the bottle of egg nog I'd polished off the night before.

"You love being my pet, don't you?" the Krampus mused, his deep voice grating over my skin, making my nipples pebble so hard they ached. "My wild little beast that I get to take out of her cage and fill and fuck and torture whenever I please. That's what you want: someone you trust to take control. All you want is a moment in time where you can be a monster's plaything and not have to worry about anything else."

He was right. It felt so...freeing.

It didn't take long for me to come around the bottle. My head fell back, my blonde hair tickling my shoulder blades as stars danced over my view of the cave's ceiling. The Krampus snickered, praising me for putting on such a delicious show.

I was snatched from the bliss when his gravelly voice returned to its harder cadence, demanding I drink the remaining fluids in the bottle.

"What?" I squeaked.

"You heard me," he growled. "You drank most of that bottle last night. Finish what you start, human. Drink."

I pulled the bottle out of me, an embarrassing wet noise filling the cave—the echo making it even more humiliating—as the seal broke between the glass and my pussy lips. There was a small mouthful of milky white fluid at the bottom of the bottle.

Closing my eyes, I brought the glass to my lips and knocked back the mouthful of fluid.

The eggnog, mixed with my juices that had leaked into the vessel, seared my tongue. It was creamy, with hints of cinnamon and something entirely my own. It was more than good. It was the perfect aphrodisiac.

"Ready for more of your punishment?"

I peered up at the Krampus and gave him an eager nod. None of this felt like a punishment, not really. It was only disguised as one, not only for his pleasure but for mine. We were both indulging in a way we never could or would with anyone else in the world.

We both knew each other's dirty secrets and here in this cave, we could let them out to breathe. To be. We could peel back each other's layers and not only appreciate the people beneath but lust for them.

Krampus snapped his fingers, and in a blink, the cage had vanished into thin air.

"Now is your chance to run."

I blinked up at him, dazed by the suggestion. Why would I run? I was having the time of my fucking life. His demonic features twisted with mock rage, and suddenly, I got the picture. "I said fucking run!"

My legs were too weak from my last mind-obliterating orgasm to get up just yet, so I crawled. I knew I wouldn't get far—neither of us had any intention of letting me escape. But I expected at least a little bit of a chase.

No such luck.

A metal collar appeared around my throat, attached to a heavy chain. He gave it a yank, and I coughed as the metal collar dug painfully into my throat, temporarily cutting off my air supply. The jerk on the leash was enough to pull my hands and knees out from under me. I went skidding belly first in the dirt.

Before I could pull myself back up, he was falling to his knees behind me. With the chain clutched tight in one claw, he gripped my hips and flipped me so I was on my back. He loomed over me, globs of saliva pearling my navel, my tits, my collar.

"I'm going to fuck you now, Clara. And since you're a naughty girl, I'm not going to warm you up with my tongue or my fingers. The bottle was the only practice you get."

I nearly choked on my own heart as it skyrocketed into my throat. *The bottle was practice?* I'd only been able to take the bottle's neck, and his cock was easily three times as girthy.

"Don't worry," he chuckled, seeing the panic flash behind my eyes. "I'll go slow."

His tongue slipped over my pussy, painting a lick over my slit to coat me with plenty of lubricant. He raised a fist, clenching the chain tight before giving it a light tug. The pulling sensation on my throat made my hips arch off the ground.

"I fucking love this little masochistic streak you've been hiding, Clara."

"And I love the goat demon you've been hiding, Bastion," I babbled through a sloppy smile as he slid his cock through my labia. My brain was on fire, imagining how the swirling ridges would feel inside me.

His hips moved back and forth to stimulate my clit with his ridges and bumps. He already felt like heaven, and he wasn't even inside me yet.

"Please," I begged, not caring how pathetic I sounded. "Put it in me. I need you inside me, Bastion."

"My naughty girl is taking her punishment so well," he praised through a fang-filled grin. "Asking so nicely for my demon cock. Be sure to scream for me, Clara."

He guided himself into my entrance with every bit of the slow pace he promised. The cage, the eggnog bottle, the leash and collar... None of it compared to the real torture of taking a giant ridged monster cock one inch at a time.

"Fuck me," I sobbed, my fingers clawing the dirt as an overwhelming amount of pleasure ravaged my entire system. The filthy, depraved bliss of it all was made that much better by the tiny shock waves of pain as he stretched me in ways no human male ever could. "Fuck, fuck, *fuck!*"

He laughed, cold and cruel, and the movement of him shaking inside me had my eyes rolling into the back of my head.

"Open your eyes," he snapped. "You're going to look the Krampus in the eye while he fucks you, naughty girl."

I opened my eyes to find a candy cane in his hand. He was sucking the end into a deadly point. A lust-drunk smile curved my lips, seeing the demon with Bastion's favorite candy. I'd been a bit worried his demon would be cruel, past the point of it being fun. But all my worries fizzled away as fuzzy warmth took its place.

Despite the horns, the crazy tongue, the hooves, the fur... It was still the mischievous man I'd come to love. The only one who'd ever seen me for who I was and urged me to be that person unapologetically. No more living a pretend life. No more fear. Just pleasure and love and lust, with a dash of dark magic and monster dong.

"Tell me you're mine, Clara," he growled as he finally buried himself inside me to the hilt. "Tell me that I'm not a stupid fool for thinking one day you'll be my wife."

"I'm yours. And you're not a fool. I'll marry you." I didn't have to think. The words fell out of me, and I meant every goddamn syllable.

He groaned his pleasure, raspy and deep. He fucked me with a rhythm that had me barreling toward yet another release in a matter of seconds. His cock was perfect. Better than any other monster cock I'd ever read about and definitely better than any human cock.

"We'll do this all the time," he gnashed out, practically reading my mind. "You'll have as much monster cock as you'll ever want or need, Clara. As my mate, I vow to keep you safe."

He arched over me, and his lips crashed down over mine in a bruising kiss. "I vow to keep you sore for as long as I have the pleasure of calling you mine."

"And how long will that be?" I giggled.

Forever. We both already knew that. But he sat back and gave his candy cane a tantalizing lick. It had a sharp point now. "For as long as you're on the naughty list, Clara."

My breath hitched when he put the candy cane to my chest, the point digging into my skin. I knew what he was about to do, and he paused, giving me a moment to parse how I felt about it. I grinned that sly smirk I'd picked up from him and nodded.

"*Scheiße*, you're perfect for me, Clara. In every way."

He kept fucking me with shallow hard thrusts as he carved into my skin with the sharpened candy cane. The cut was shallow but deep enough to draw blood. I wanted to look and tried craning my neck to see what he'd carved into my flesh.

He snarled a warning and jerked on my chain. "You get to look when you come for me, Clara. Come around the Krampus' cock. I want to feel your cream coat me as you scream your pleasure, naughty girl."

He came first. Thick torrents of cum filled me, and when I couldn't hold another drop more, it leaked down the swells of my ass, soaking into the dirt floor beneath us. I felt so full, so filthy. Every bit the naughty girl I was.

With that, I came violently. It crashed over me like a crushing tidal wave, robbing me of my ability to breathe for several intense seconds. I gasped for breath while he praised me through his pleasure-laced huffs.

He pulled gently on the chain with one hand, and with his other, he cupped my head, lifting it off the ground so I could see his handy work.

In bloody letters, he'd carved the word "Naughty" into my chest. Little beads of blood pooled between my breasts, creating a beautifully gruesome sight that would be branded onto my brain forever.

He pushed the candy cane into my mouth and sat back on his haunches to appreciate the scene. "Fucking perfect…"

"Merry Christmas, Bastion," I hummed.

There was that grin again I loved so damn much. The one he'd only ever given me and no one else. I wasn't sure how I missed how much love he'd always packed into it, even when we were kids.

"Merry Christmas, little beast."


THE END

# Epilogue

## Clara

“Thank you for shopping at Floral Wonderland.”

Bastion’s customer service voice was interrupted by a growl, followed by a curse. “*Verdammt!*”

I strode out of the back office to find my husband trying to pack a customer’s purchase into a bag with one hand while struggling to hold our squirmy baby in the other.

“You’re lucky Holly doesn’t speak German yet, Bast.” I laughed softly, watching our almost one-year-old daughter sliding down her daddy’s hip. She looked so cute in her red Christmas jumper, white stockings and baby Mary Jane’s.

"Here, let me help." I walked behind the counter, took the indoor plant food from Bastion, placed it in the bag, and handed it to the waiting customer.

They left with a smile and a "Happy Holidays" before disappearing into the snowy night with a jingle of the bells hanging from the front door.

"About ready to close up for Christmas Eve, Mrs. Weber?"

I smiled, kissing his candy-sweet lips. "*Scheiße, ja.*"

He grinned at my reply. "Out of all the German I've tried to teach you, of course, it's the curse words you remember."

I stuck out my tongue at him with a wink before grabbing my purse and brandishing the store keys. "The curse words are all you need with the Krampus as your personal translator."

It had been over a year since that fateful Christmas in the Krampus cave. To this day, I was still his first and only victim. Instead of terrorizing naughty villagers or succumbing to his demon's desires, he focused on the shop and being the partner I deserved.

He sold his land and tree farm, giving up his dad's dream to buy back my mother's old ornament shop. The old building I'd adored since I was little was finally mine.

I'd spent years staring out of my old shop window, gazing at the building across the street and daydreaming about the life I'd one day have.

Now I had all that and so much more.

I no longer had to pretend my life was perfect. It really was.

My florist shop was now in my dream location, where I felt closest to my mom. We had a beautiful baby girl who would one day inherit her father's "curse." She would be the first female Krampus in generations.

And the best part: I was free to be myself, whether that meant snuggling on the couch with my Bastion and Holly while watching old holiday specials or sneaking off to the cave to reenact the best Christmas ever.

I was now convinced Christmas miracles really could happen—dark and bloody ones rooted in ancient magic.

Even if it was a miracle as simple as a book, reminding the reader that if the hero is taking his sweet time saving her, it's okay.

In the end, *Clara saves herself.*

# About the Author

Aiden Pierce is a writer of dark paranormal romance and erotic horror. Her love stories are on the spooky side and usually end up with the monster or the villain getting the girl. She lives in the Pacific Northwest with her husband and their three fur babies.

You can find Aiden on any of these platforms:
Instagram —> @aidenpierceromance
TikTok —> @aidenpierceromance
Her website —> www.authoraidenpierce.com